Finding Joy
in Pain

Finding Joy in Pain

Roslyn M. Wyche-Hamilton

URBAN BOOKS
http://www.urbanbooks.net

URBAN SOUL is published by

Urban Books
1199 Straight Path
West Babylon, NY 11704

ISBN-13: 978-1-59983-089-6
ISBN-10: 1-59983-089-2

First Printing: March 2009

10 9 8 7 6 5 4 3 2 1

Printed in the United States of America

Acknowledgments

Wow! I finally finished my first novel. I would like to thank, first and foremost, my Lord and savior. None of this would be possible without you. Next, I would like to thank my family and friends for believing in me. To Guy, Jaz, and Guy Jr., thanks for your patience and support. To my two miracles, Jaz and Boy Boy, words can never express the overwhelming love, admiration, and devotion I have for you.

To my parents, thanks for allowing me the freedom to be creative and eccentric at times. Mom (Joyce), you have such a beautiful spirit and I love you. To my Dad (Arthur), although you are gone, you will always be in my heart and on my mind. I miss you! Tell all of my peeps up there that I said hi.

To the Wyche, Hamilton, Smith, Norman, and Davis families, thanks! To my brothers Slim and Trevis, smooches! To baby sis, Gigi, you are and always will be my little live doll baby. To my nieces and nephews! I expect nothing but great things from you. Make sure your education stays your number one priority. Uncle Bill, thanks for taking me to college when I needed a ride. Wow, my family is too big! Too many to name (so sorry). I still love you guys!

To my little cousins, I love you all! The rest of your kids and their kids; To my sister/cousins: Meloney, thanks for all of your input. Vernell, thanks for listening and being there for me!

To my mother-in-law, Bea . . . just because. To my brothers-in-law and sisters-in-law, thanks! To my father-in-law, thanks.

To my Del State family, I will see you at homecoming. There are just too many to mention. You know who you are.

To my church family, keep praying for me!!

To my goddaughters: Tamara, I'm so proud of you. Enjoy your college experience. Eboni, my future fashion designer, reach for the stars! Queen, you're our other little princess!

Where my Sorors at? To the women of Delta Sigma Theta, you're the best!

To my book-club girls and longtime friends, SOS, Zee, Monique, Robin, Rose, Gia, Kim, and Judy, thanks for making the book club interesting and thanks for the bangin' food and drinks. At times, it was crazy, but what do you expect? You know how we do!

Special shout-outs go to Rosanne, Dar (my co-ordinator for life), Khia S., Anne, Elisha J.,

Teresa, Steve Y., Nay Nay, Ashley, Tracey, Joy, Carla, Zatanya, Felicia D., Adrian, Trish, Rodney, Dawn, Buster, Rus, Jill, Tracey V., Sean, Pierre, Caliek, Christal, Donna B., Adam, Matt, Aunt Teetie, Vonnie, Terrean, Julia, Keisha, Lovell, Chantel, Flip, Toyya, Stacy H., Gina, Shante, Linda M., Mary, Lottie, Aesha, Shelly, Valerie, Ms. Shirley & Tamara, and Julia Hunter. Thank you so much for everything.

To my agent, Maxine Thompson, thank you for your time and patience. Your words of encouragement and kind words of inspiration motivated me to continue on! Thanks to the publishing company for the opportunity to do what I love to do.

And last but not least, to everyone else I failed to mention, don't blame my heart, just my mind. Just let me know, and I will make sure I don't forget you in the next book.

Peace

Prologue

What a beautiful day for a wedding! The super-stretched Navigator and Lexus limousines were parked out front, where the chauffeurs patiently stood, waiting to assist the bridal party.

The wedding took place outside, overlooking the hills and valleys. The scenery was beautiful, and the weather was perfect. The coordinator had white chairs and red roses set up everywhere. There was an older, distinguished gentleman on the saxophone, playing Brian McKnight's "Never Felt This Way" as the guests arrived to take their seats. The women guests were greeted with a single red rose and escorted to their seats.

"Ouch! That guy stepped on my foot and didn't have the decency to say excuse me," Miss Nelly, the bride's godmother, complained. One of the guests had mistakenly stepped on her foot on his way to his seat. In all fairness to him, Miss Nelly had kind of been in his way.

"Who stepped on your foot?" asked the hostess.

"That man over there, with the Zorro-looking outfit and black hat on, looking like a fake R. Kelly, 'Step in the Name of Love' wannabe."

"Miss Nelly, you are so crazy," laughed the hostess.

"No, I'm not crazy. But if he steps on my toes again, I will show you crazy."

All the guests had received a program to follow along during the ceremony. The wedding programs were quite exquisite and classy; they were decorated with white crepe paper and gold tassels. They also featured embossed gold lettering, which you could actually feel and read, with your eyes closed, if you rubbed your fingers across the words.

Also present were a beautiful white carriage and horse. The horse was actually real and obviously very hungry. It seemed to enjoy munching on the grass. The coordinator, on the other hand, looked as though she could stand to miss a meal or two. She appeared to be going just a tad bit crazy. She hurriedly walked around, carrying two white doves in a small cage, while talking into a headset. It was obvious that she was stressing over the wedding.

The parking lot was jam-packed. It seemed as though anybody who was somebody was present. You could see and hear all the excited guests, dressed in their best attire. Of course, you had the people who wanted to outdress the bride and groom. They looked like they were stepping out to attend the Grammy Awards. The photographer and video guy had just finished setting up their equipment. The guests had been seated. The groom and best man stood quietly. The saxophonist continued to play as the members of the bridal party took their places. The coordinator finally sat down. The pastor looked up and nodded. Everyone stood up. Now it was time to get started . . . Here comes the bride.

Chapter 1

The Wedding

Joi

Finally, the day I, Joi Nicole Thompson, would be forced to remember for the rest of my life was here. Today was July 18. Damn! Exactly twenty-eight days from the time I had received my invitation to Jay's wedding. And it had taken me twenty-one days to respond. Today I would watch my one true love marry someone else. As far as I was concerned, this was the worst day of my life. I had always been a glutton for punishment. The traffic on the New Jersey Turnpike was hectic. I had to drive almost two hours from Secaucus, New Jersey, to get to Jaylen's wedding, which was taking place near his home in the suburbs of Philadelphia. Luckily, the wedding and the reception were at the same location, because the drive was somewhat long, and I was tired. I knew I should have come a day earlier. However, I was attending a work-related seminar, and I was in no mood to drive that great a distance by myself in the middle of the night.

The navigation system on my vehicle guided me directly to the location of the wedding ceremony. There was a male attendant directing all guests to park their vehicles in the underground parking lot across the street. As I got out of my car, my nerves started to get the best of me.

Why am I here? I must be crazy.

From this moment, it felt like I was losing a part of myself. I might as well be attending a funeral today, because I'd been crying all morning, and now my eyes were red and puffy. I just had to get myself together before this wedding. I needed to be happy for him no matter what. Toni was so lucky, because Jaylen was a good man. He was black, educated, over six feet tall, and straight. Hmm, that was more than half the battle. But on top of that, he was so fine and so sexy. His caramel complexion, pretty teeth, neatly trimmed mustache, and goatee had always turned me on. Besides being tall, slim, and athletic, he dressed his ass off. Trust me. He had it going on. I had messed up. This might have been my biggest mistake ever.

On my way to the wedding, my mind echoed, *This bitch has my man.* I'm *supposed to be his wife, not* her. That was just the way I felt. He was truly my soul mate, my college sweetheart, and I'd known him for half of my life. We had just chosen different career paths, and when he'd asked me to marry him five years ago, I hadn't been ready. We remained close and always kept in touch. He had even asked me to give it one more chance and to further explore our feelings, but I'd been involved with someone else at the time. I knew we loved each other, but our timing was always off. It took me up to this day to realize just how much I missed and loved him.

The guests had arrived and had already taken their seats. I went inside and met up with Faith, Taj, and Eboni. The mother of the bride and the parents of the groom were seated in the front row. The bride's father was with the rest of the bridal party, waiting to walk his daughter down the aisle. The band was playing a jazz selection by Gerald Albright as the wedding party made its way down the aisle, along with the flower girl and ring bearer. The bridesmaids wore peach designer gowns with three-inch cream sling-back sandals, and the groomsmen wore black tuxedos with peach cummerbunds, cream shirts, black shoes, and bow ties. The entire wedding party looked really nice.

"Will everyone please stand," announced the coordinator.

Here she comes, I thought, wondering what she looked like. Her father proudly served as her escort. *Mmm, she is taking entirely too long to walk down the aisle.* Finally, I saw her face. She wasn't all that bad, but not nearly what I had expected. I was just trying to keep it real. She stood about five feet eight, was slim, and had a light brown complexion. She wore her hair straight down, with a white rose on one side. Her hair was black, and she had dark, mysterious eyes. She wore a stylish white dress with a plunging neckline. It had the appearance of a plain white dress from a distance, but when I saw it up close, it was fierce. It looked like something out of Kimora Lee Simmons's closet. I didn't know where she had got that dress, but I wanted one, just maybe in another color. As she walked down the aisle, I heard a familiar song being softly piped in through the outdoor speakers.

Wow. I cannot believe they're playing this song as their wedding song! This song was supposed to be our song—mine and Jaylen's!

That did it! I was outdone. He had the audacity to sing some of the lyrics to her as she made her way down the aisle. He acted as though it was some personal dedication or tribute.

"I hope he chokes on those words," I muttered.

The bride-to-be finally made her way all the way down the aisle and grabbed Jaylen's hand. She gazed into Jaylen's eyes, and they both shared a brief yet endearing smile. My best friend, Faith, who was standing to my right, nudged me in an effort to get my attention.

"Joi? Look at Jay. He's crying," she blurted.

"So what, Faith? Who cares?" I did. The nerve of him crying, knowing I was there and how I felt about the situation. It was completely pissing me off. I didn't know why I'd agreed to come to this wedding. What the hell had I been thinking? Maybe I'd thought Jaylen would see me at the wedding and realize that he just could not go through with it.

The wedding officiant was a woman by the name of Dr. Lorena Hart. She was dressed in African garb. Not my style, but, hey! Whatever floats your boat! She spoke with an abundance of emotion. I guess you could say she was a female version of Dr. Martin Luther King Jr. I kept thinking she was going to say, "I had a dream that one day . . ." Anyway, you get my point. She took forever saying whatever it was that she needed to say. I could tell she was very impressed with herself. But then again, she did have a doctorate degree, and I was all about education.

"Ladies and gentlemen, Toni and Jaylen have decided to exchange their own personal wedding vows," Dr. Hart announced.

What! I screamed inside. *I can't handle this!*

Jaylen spoke very softly. I could barely hear him, which was good, and every now and then, he would pat his chest. I guess it helped him get through his vows, which appeared to be very sincere; then again, he could have just had a bad case of heartburn.

"Toni, I knew the first time that I saw you that you were the one. You are my life. . . ."

Oh, hell, no!! I know he didn't even go there. He

had always told me that I was his everything, and that no one could ever replace me.

From that point on, everything else just seemed to fade. I just wanted him to shut the hell up. He had a lot of nerve parting his lips to utter those words. He had told me how they met. He had seen her at a club, and they had danced, exchanged numbers, and eventually started dating. As time went on, the relationship got a little more serious. Jaylen had mentioned on a few occasions that Toni had a demanding job, but he would never reveal her occupation. I never asked, because he obviously did not want me to know, and I could have cared less. Anyway, she convinced him to move out of his apartment and into her home. The rest was history.

Now it was her turn. She was Jamaican, which would explain the overwhelming confidence she displayed, as if she were auditioning for a part as the actual Statue of Liberty. She had the "extra" personality thing going on.

"I wrote mine on a piece of paper so that I won't forget anything. Jay, I love you for so many reasons. You are funny, smart, and handsome. I promise you today that I will communicate with you, respect and love you. You are everything a woman could ask for in a mate, and I consider myself lucky enough to have found someone like you to share my life with. You have given me the faith to believe in love again. . . ."

Yada, yada, yada. I did not know you picked your wedding day to start communicating, respecting, and loving your partner. Didn't you get married after all these qualities had been demonstrated? It was obvious that she didn't have a clue. She had just put on the dress and shown up. Besides, this was her second marriage and his first. The fact that she had to write her wedding vows down on a piece of paper clearly told me a lot, or maybe she had whipped out a copy of her old vows from her first marriage. I could have delivered my wedding vows to him straight from the heart, looking him dead in the eye, without a blink in sight, until I was done. Because when you knew someone and truly loved him, it just happened naturally.

They exchanged their rings, and now it was time to make it official by hearing those dreadful words.

"I now pronounce you husband and wife. You may kiss your bride," said Dr. Hart.

I mentally passed out. *Somebody please call 911.* After they kissed, he gave his identical twin brother, Jordan, the best man, a high five, along with the other two groomsmen. Everyone laughed except me. I was even pissed off at Faith, Taj, and Eboni, because they seemed to be enjoying this wedding. They were snapping pictures, and complimenting and hugging the bride and groom a bit too much. *Mental note. Kick Faith's, Taj's, and Eboni's hoochie asses to the curb tomorrow. I can't wait for them to be in my shoes. I might just be in their exes' weddings and let* them see how that shit felt. If you couldn't hurt with me when I was hurting, I didn't need you.

Jaylen had invited Faith, Taj, and Eboni to the wedding because we had all been close friends in college. I guess he knew I would need them for moral support, but I definitely had not expected them to have this much fun. I was much closer to Faith, because we had grown up together like sisters and our families were close. Eboni had been my roommate in college, while Faith and Taj had been roommates. We had partied together, pledged the same sorority together, dated guys within the same clique. At times, it had been a bit much. We just hung out together all the time, and when we graduated, we all moved to the same area in New Jersey.

Now it was time to hear those dreadful words.

"And for the first time, ladies and gentlemen, I introduce to you Mr. and Mrs. Jaylen Payne." *Mr. and Mrs. Jaylen Payne . . . Mr. and Mrs. Jaylen Payne . . .*

I finally snapped out of it, and everyone was clapping. Of course, I clapped, because it seemed as though all eyes were on me, even though I was sure I was overexaggerating. I clapped for what I thought was a sufficient amount of time, and then I quickly stopped.

The wedding ceremony was finally over, and the reception was just beginning. Luckily, I had purchased a card the day before. I usually ran out and grabbed a card in between the wedding and the reception. I was prepared today.

The card was pretty basic. The outside read *For The Bride & Groom,* and the inside read *Congratulations!* I had written a check for one hundred dollars. I could have made it for more, but I did not feel the need to prove anything to anybody.

"There will be a brief cocktail hour for the guests to enjoy while the bridal party meets in the garden for pictures. Everyone else can go out in the ballroom for some hors d'oeuvres and cocktails," announced the coordinator.

I found my seat, which was close and right in the front. Instead of numbered tables, they had chosen to use themes. They had selected words like *Serenity, Peace, Love, Beautiful,* and so forth. I was at the "Beautiful" table, along with Taj, Faith, and Eboni. We sat with some of Jaylen's relatives from Texas and with a couple from Jamaica who knew the bride. My aunt Alexis was supposed to come, but she had left a message on my cell, saying she was not feeling well.

From the moment we arrived inside the ballroom, I could tell Jaylen was slightly nervous about coming over to speak to me. Every time he got nervous, he ran his hands over his goatee and licked his lips. He must have done it a dozen times. Every time I looked up, I would catch him glancing in my direction. I didn't want to keep staring at him, so I focused my energy on the decorations. The room was beautiful and elegant. The lights were dim, and the room was filled with exotic-looking flowers. Finally, he made his way to our table.

"Hello, ladies. Thanks for coming. You all look very nice," Jaylen said.

He then bent down, kissed me on my cheek, and whispered in my ear, "Especially you." I could smell the scent of his cologne. He was wearing my favorite, Man, by Calvin Klein. I wanted to reach up and throw my arms around him and never let go. It was killing me inside. It was like someone had ripped out my heart and tossed it out the damn window. It wasn't a good feeling. Anyway, he chatted briefly and left.

"Girl, that man was lookin' good," Eboni said while stomping her feet.

"Girlfriend, please stop sweating my ex," I grumbled.

"Sorry, Joi. I had to give the brotha some props. No disrespect intended," Eboni replied.

"As long as you know," I said.

I was smiling, but it was obvious that I had an issue with Eboni's comment. I finally regained my composure and appreciated his compliment. At least he had noticed my efforts. I must say, I was looking good. At least I thought so. I wore a dress designed by Nanette Lepore, which I had purchased at Nordstrom. It was a silk orange and brown halter dress with metallic straps and beading. The length was slightly above the knee, which allowed the dress to show off my legs. I had accented the dress with some three-inch chocolate brown tie-up sandals. I wore some Betsey Johnson silver drop earrings and one of her slamming bracelets, which showed off my manicured fingers and delicate wrists, just to drive him crazy. My hair was layered in a blunt shoulder-length cut with subtle highlights. I did not want my hair to look too dramatic. The length was perfect: it flattered my shoulders, and it bounced with every turn. Hmm, I felt like America's next top model. My friends didn't look bad themselves, and together, we all knew how to turn heads.·

Taj was tall and slim. She had a light cocoa brown complexion with almond shaped eyes. Taj was a Juicy Couture girl. She wore a sharp baby blue pants outfit. Her jacket had the J-Lo signature front. She had her breasts neatly inside the jacket, and the middle was wide open. It looked over-the-top sexy and too edgy for me. Her hair was in braids, and she wore them straight down her back. Taj worked part time as a model and also as a manager at Club Phaze.

Eboni had her own look. She reminded me of Chilli from the group TLC, except she was shorter and darker. Eboni had to be mixed with something, yet she always insisted that she was 100 percent black. Her hair was pinned up and accented with decorative Asian chopsticks. She wore a peach dress with a portion of the shoulder out, along with some peach, yellow, and white Gucci sling-backs, with a Horsebit bag to match. Eboni kept up with the latest fashions since she was an A&R manager at her father's record company. She kept it conservative, though. She kept a Juicy Couture or a

Dooney & Bourke bag in her wardrobe at all times. Her family was rich, and she really didn't have to work. But I was glad she did, because she always had the hookup.

Faith was medium height, brown skinned, and her hair was cut into a short platinum blond do. She wore a sleeveless mint green jumpsuit with some silver sandals and a matching Coach bag. She was so fly and down to earth. Faith was still in school, finishing up her nursing degree. She had already started interviewing for jobs, because she was set to graduate in a couple of months. Her other love was poetry, and every now and then, she would recite one or two at an open mic. She spoke her poetry from the heart. Sometimes, I would shake my head in disbelief and laugh because Faith would snap out with her poetry, if she needed to. I remember one time she caught her man in her bed with a trick, and she flipped out. Afterwards, she decided to share her ordeal with everyone at the open mic. It was called "Ain't that a Bitch!!"

> *Oh, hell, no! I know my man ain't in the bed with this ho.*
> *My first instinct was to snap . . . Yeah, snap her f-in' neck and slice off his shit.*
> *Toss it in the garbage disposal and flick the switch!! Ouch. Ain't that a bitch. . . .*
> *They wasn't gonna find that piece and sew it back on. That thing is long gone!*

What the hell were they thinking, knowing I
  would go off?
Didn't they know my ass was on Zoloft?
I reached for my drawer to grab me a weapon,
  changed my mind quickly, and recited a prayer
  in five seconds. My insides were crumbling,
  and I kept imagining this vision. I knew this
  would be a mind-blowing decision.
Physically I stood, yet emotionally I was falling
  apart. My mind remained strong, while this
  asshole was breaking my heart.
Screwin' this stank, lonely bitch in my bed . . .
  Whew, unrepeatable thoughts were going
  through my head.
I decided through it all that I was so much better
  than that . . . Damn, this scene is whacked!
So I walked out and left their naked asses behind,
  but not before I dropped a bomb to blow their
  f-in' minds. Ain't that a bitch!

She was so emotional and the crowd was feeling her so much that they gave her a standing ovation. The sistas in the room were throwing their hands in the air, snapping their fingers, and yelling. "You go, girl. You're my shero," one shouted. I didn't even think that they knew her poem was from a personal experience. It was her way of expressing herself, instead of telling you about yourself. It was her outlet.

Earlier that day, we had bumped into this lady in the parking lot. She was about five feet three and had a medium brown complexion, and her hair was pulled back in a ponytail. She had on a multicolored flowered dress and a straw hat and sandals. Everywhere we went, she was right there. She stared at us and examined us from head to toe. I later found out that she was a relative of the bride.

We got up to get something to eat and bumped right into Jaylen and his wife, Toni. I introduced myself to her, and she surprisingly said, "Joi!" as if to indicate that she was overly anxious to meet me and had just heard so much about me. The truth of the matter was she could not wait to check out what she thought was possible competition, because I had hung up on her about five months ago. It had not been intentional. I'd been calling Jay, and he'd told me he turned his cell off after 6 p.m., but I could leave a message. I'd called him around 7 p.m., and she'd answered, and I'd hung up!! He'd called me right back. I'd apologized and explained to him that I just had not expected her to answer, and it had thrown me off guard. He'd said he understood. He told me that she would throw my name up in his face from time to time and wondered why I never called them at the home phone number. I had it, but I never felt the need to use it. Besides, I knew what we shared in the past and how I still felt, and my calling their home would have been disrespectful and somewhat pretentious.

Anyway, I gave both of them hugs, and when Jaylen's hands touched my back, I could have melted. Not only did his hands feel good, he was looking good. For a split second, I imagined him and me sneaking off into the parking lot somewhere for one final good-bye. Nah! Just like it says in R. Kelly's song, he was the best sex I had ever had. I started having flashbacks of every romantic tryst we ever had and when we used to take lovemaking to another level.

"I can't believe this. Here we are at this classy-ass wedding, and there is no open bar," I said, instantly sounding annoyed.

In a way, I understood. I guessed the bride and groom wanted to control the consumption of alcohol to ensure that some of the guests would not get inebriated.

I needed to go and get some fresh air quick, fast, and in a hurry. I was starting to hyperventilate. Taj, Faith, Eboni, and I decided that we would go outside to the truck and drink our Alizé, because they had a cash bar at the wedding.

"Ladies, I need to go to the powder room first to freshen up. After that, we can go outside. Are you guys coming or not?" Taj asked.

"Yes, Taj, we're coming. Our hair and makeup need some immediate attention," said Faith.

"Nah, Taj. I'm stressin'. I'll just meet you, Faith, and Eboni at the truck in a few. Besides, y'alls hair look tore up from the floor up. I'm kidding. I owed you one," I said.

"That's cool, Joi. Go and get your laugh on at our expense. However, know this. It won't be funny if you forget to save us something to drink," said Taj.

It was so hot outside, but I needed some fresh air. My truck was parked in the underground lot across the street from the reception. I walked across the street and headed toward my vehicle.

"Where are my keys?" I muttered to myself. I searched around in my purse until I found them.

"Did you find what you were looking for?" asked a familiar male voice.

I looked up, and there he was, standing on the opposite side of my vehicle.

"Jay! You scared me. Don't sneak up on me like that, and why are you out here?"

"I followed you."

"Why?"

"I'm not sure," he said.

It seemed like something was heavy on his mind and he needed to talk to me about it. I walked around my truck to get the Alizé out of the cooler.

"Joi, I miss you," he blurted out.

"Where is this coming from Jaylen? You just said I do to another woman."

"Baby, I know none of this makes sense right now, but I feel like I made a mistake. Joi, look at me. We've been through thick and thin together. I just cannot imagine us with other people. I know this looks bad, but we can get through this. I know I just married Toni, but the whole time I was thinking about you."

"Jaylen, how in the hell am I supposed to react?"

"Joi Nicole, I love you and I'm sorry. I made a mistake."

Damn, damn, damn!! *I said to myself. "Well, I guess it's a bit too late to confess now. You just got married. I'm happy for you. . . ."*

Before I knew it, he started kissing me and leaning me on the edge of my truck. I couldn't stop him.

"Jay, I can't do this. It isn't right."

He managed to slide the top part of my dress down past my shoulders, and I just couldn't control myself any further.

Lord, help me. I still love this man, *I thought.*

He was all over me. Knowing my weakness, he pushed me backwards, exposing my breasts. He was kissing me behind my ears and on my neck. I knew at this point I was done, because all I had on was a black thong under my dress. I then took off his tuxedo jacket and laid it down in the SUV. I was unbuttoning his shirt and zipping down his pants as fast as I could. He climbed up on top of me and started kissing me again. I grabbed the back of his head and started kissing him back. He slowly lifted my leg and snapped off my thong and tossed it over the seat.

I knew he was about to make his grand entry. I just didn't expect it so quickly. He started forcing every inch inside of me even before my thong landed. He wanted to make sure he reminded me of what I was missing. I wanted to scream, but all I could do was hold on to him since he had full control over me. The truck was rocking forward, backward, and sideways. We didn't have a lot of room, but he worked me over until I couldn't move. I was outdone! He still had it going on. I must have come a few times. My dress was still attached by one leg, and my hair was all over. I didn't want us to get busted, so we had to get up. We put on our clothes as fast as we could. Both of my legs were trembling, and my ass was hurting. I knew he missed me, and I missed him, because we were both crying and holding on to each other.

"Joi! Joi! Joi! Girl, I know you heard us calling you," Faith yelled.

"I know this heffa hears me calling her name, and she isn't even responding. What's up with that?" Eboni questioned.

"Where did you drift off to? Did you drink all of the Alizé?" Taj asked.

"Girl, I'm tripping. I fell off into la-la land. I was truly buggin', and no, I did not drink all of the Alizé," I said.

Eboni poured some Alizé into our cups, and I told her all about it. It had seemed so real. I tried to tell them that Jaylen had followed me out to the truck, and Eboni just laughed and said, "Aww, Joi, you're going through a bad time. Maybe it was a bad idea to come."

"Joi, you are losing it," Faith whispered while hugging me.

"I'm cool. I'm just feeling some kind of way. I'll be fine. I hope," I said in a tearful voice.

"We know you will be just fine," Eboni said.

"How could he marry her?" I cried.

Taj and Eboni managed to catch me before I fell completely apart.

"Honey, it's his loss. Please don't cry. You're going to make me cry," Faith said in a sad tone.

"I'm cool. I'm hurt, and I just feel so stupid. I came to share another woman's daydream with Jaylen, which makes it my nightmare. I thought I could handle this, but I can't. I'll be fine . . . I hope," I said in a tearful voice.

Taj and Eb caught me before I fell apart again.

"Shake it off, Joi. Shake it off. Go like this," Taj said while she moved her body in a bad version of the Harlem shake. We all had a group hug. *Mental note. Don't kick my girls to the curb, because they got my back, after all.*

Now we made our way back to the reception. The bride and groom were ready to have their first dance.

Oh, Lord, here we go again, I silently complained to myself.

It was almost like Toni had hired her coordinator to personally follow me and start shit up as soon as I showed my face. I envisioned the coordinator on a walkie-talkie, with her assistant saying, "Here she comes, code Ex. Let's start the first dance, over." They should have been done with the toast and first dance. Shit, they should have already been on a flight to their honeymoon destination.

Anyway, the bride chose her own song, and the groom chose his. I didn't even remember the names of the songs. Thank God it was over within ten minutes.

"I am starving. Where is the food?" I whined. It was bad enough the wedding had started late; now we had to wait forever to eat. Finally, the waiter made his way over to our table with a salad, but not enough ranch dressing.

"Excuse me, sir. Can we have some more ranch dressing? We ran out," Faith politely asked.

The waiter replied, "I'll bring some out in a minute." It must have taken him twenty minutes or more. The hostess had already started serving us our food when he returned with the dressing.

"Oh, boy, what a big carrot stick with the little green thingies on it. It looks good, and if it ain't, I'll eat it, anyway, because I'm hungry!" I said. "I hate crunchy string beans. I want some soul food. I am in the mood for some barbe-cued ribs, macaroni and cheese, collard greens, and some sweet potato cheesecake." *Mental note to self. If and when I do get married, I will have some soul food at my reception.*

The menu consisted of chicken stuffed with spinach in a tomato sauce, scalloped potatoes, carrot sticks, and string beans. I tried to finish everything on my plate, but apparently my eyes were bigger than my stomach.

Clink . . . clink . . . clink. The best man was about to make his speech. "I would just like to take this opportunity to say that I wish my brother the best in whatever he decides in life. It takes a very special woman to take care of my brother. Congratulations, Jaylen and Toni."

Everyone clapped. I knew Jordan wasn't

feeling his brother's choice of a bride. He had
told me on several occasions. We were very
close. But he wanted to support his brother's
decision and be there for him. I understood.

I wanted a piece of cake, but I couldn't remember whether or not they were having the
cake-cutting ceremony. "Hell, who cares? I'll
cut the cake my damn self. I might just go and
smash a piece in the bride's face. I'm tipsy, and
I don't care," I announced.

Just then the DJ shouted over the mic, "Are
y'all ready to party?"

"Hell yeah," yelled Taj and Eboni.

"It's about time, and they better play something we can party off of. You know the first
record is just so important," I said in a demanding tone.

Everybody started jumping up to dance to
Beyoncé's new song.

"Oh, boy, here comes Jay," I mumbled.

"Come on, Joi. May I please have this dance?"
Jaylen asked while extending his right hand
to me.

"No, I don't want to dance right now, Jaylen.
I was just about to go and get me a piece of
cake," I replied.

"Come on, Joi," he said.

"I don't want to dance right now," I repeated.

He continued to drag me to the dance floor.
I really did want to dance with him, but I was
only hatin'. Besides, I loved this record. After
a lot of tugging and pleading, I decided to

dance with him to prevent any further stares. We danced and talked.

"I can't believe you were giving me such a hard time over a dance," he said.

"I just did not want to dance at that particular second."

"Okay. But seriously, I'm glad you came. I just wish things could have worked out different."

"Yeah, I guess."

For a brief moment, it was as if Jaylen was having second thoughts about his marriage to Toni. I started to ask what he meant when he said he wished things could have worked out differently, but I decided to leave well enough alone.

"Well, I just figured that since I danced with my wife on the first slow record, I had to dance with you off of the first fast record," said Jaylen.

I started to laugh. His comment was a little crazy, but it kept me from breaking down and crying again. At one point, we even did a little dance we used to do back in the day. For a moment, I acted as if I was the bride, until reality hit me in the face again. I could not help but notice his parents looking over at us. They had that "we wish you two were married today" look.

Stop trippin', Joi, I told myself. *It's over, so deal with it.*

I just figured that if you couldn't beat them, join them. I decided to start a Soul Train line, which was a tradition of mine. I resolved to do the cabbage patch to put everybody in the old-school mind-set. Everyone was trying to make it down the line and get their turn, but those damn kids just stayed in the way. Of course, it looked cute at first, but they refused to move down the line so that the rest of us could get our party on.

Mental note . . . if and when I get married, adult reception only.

"I can't believe the DJ just played Michael Jackson's song 'Wanna Be Startin' Somethin',"" I openly complained.

The same thing had happened when I went to Club Dream. They had Michael Jackson playing on the first, second, third, and fourth floor. Don't get me wrong. I loved Mike, but timing was everything. I was trying to get my party on. The only way the DJ could exonerate himself was to play the cha-cha slide, and I basically threatened him so that he would play it. And when he finally played it, I couldn't wait to hop, reverse, and break it down.

The night was ending, and people were starting to leave. I searched around the room for Jaylen so that I could say good-bye. Toni sat near the door, as if she was looking for him also. So, we just said our good-byes and left. I drove back home and sat in my car for a few minutes. I wanted to try to get rid of some residual feelings I had left inside of me. I turned on a song by Eric Benet and played it at least three times at max volume. I wanted to cry, but I couldn't. Jaylen had moved on with his life, and I needed to do the same. I knew going to this wedding would hurt, but I hadn't expected it to hurt this much. Regardless, our relationship was over. Faith called me on my cell to see if I had made it home safely and to see how I was doing. I reassured her that I was okay. After that, we hung up the phone, and I went to the kitchen to make a cup of tea. I took a nice long shower and eventually fell asleep. *Alone.*

Chapter 2

The Honeymoon

Jaylen

My wife and I arrived at the airport at 7:30 a.m. We had decided to take a cruise to the Bahamas for our honeymoon. I had never been on a cruise before, but I had heard it was nice. Toni was more in tune with which cruise lines were considered top-notch, so I had let her make the reservations. After weeks of searching, she'd booked a seven-day trip with the cruise line Royal Caribbean. We had to fly from Philadelphia to Miami. Once we arrived in Miami, we were greeted by employees of Royal Caribbean with fancy drinks and Calypso-style music. Afterwards, we were taken to the pier so that we could gain entrance to the ship. The ship was huge, and it was called *Majesty of the Sea*. There were people everywhere. They were on the top deck and the main deck. Toni was busy soaking up all the ship had to offer. She seemed excited about going shopping, dancing, and to the casino.

"Oh, Jaylen, this is just what we needed. A seven-day cruise to the Bahamas," Toni cooed. "I can't wait to see our cabin. It's the honeymoon suite. I hope you like it."

"Well, let's go check in first. I'm pretty anxious to see what our cabin looks like. Afterwards, we can take a tour."

"Jay, can you please remind me to get some postcards while we are out? I want to send them out to my family and friends. You might want to grab a few to send out, also."

"No thanks. I'm good. I see my family and friends enough. They don't need any postcards from me. I already shared my wedding with them, so I prefer to keep my honeymoon memories to myself."

"Well, I thought you might want to send one to your brother or maybe even to Joi," Toni said in a slightly sarcastic tone.

"Now why would I do that? My brother, Jordan, could care less and Joi . . ."

"And Joi what, Jaylen?" Toni asked.

"Joi has better things to do than read a postcard from me," I said.

"I bet she does."

"Look, Toni, I did not come here to talk about Joi. My life is with you, and that's all we should be discussing. Joi and I are friends, and we share a past. It's no different than your past with your ex-husband, Kenyatta."

"I was just thinking that a postcard might cheer her up. I was not trying to insinuate anything. I couldn't help but notice that she looked so sad at our wedding."

"What gave you the impression that she was sad? Maybe she was tired or something," I replied.

"What do you mean by 'or something,' Jay?" asked Toni.

"Here we go again. You're trippin', and I refuse to go there with you."

"You're right. Please accept my apology."

It was apparent that Toni was feeling threatened by Joi, because she brought her name up on a daily basis. It was like she was obsessed. Maybe I gave her a reason to feel insecure. Although I did love my wife, I would always care for Joi. My connection with her was pure and natural. I remembered how we could just go to the beach and sit there for hours. We could talk about anything. I mean anything. I would disagree with her, and she would disagree with me. There was a high degree of mutual respect between us. However, Toni and I were different. She was a good person, and I did love her. She was attractive, educated, and a hell of a good cook. Her only downfall was her personality. One minute she was great to be around, and the next minute she was complaining about everything. Toni had graduated from

Spelman College eight years ago, with a degree in information technology, and she worked for Myteck Inc.

My mom was from the old school. Although my mom liked Toni, she seemed to think that our relationship had moved way too fast. She knew I'd been hurt when Joi and I went our separate ways. I had pretty much shut myself down and thrown all my energy into my company. I had worked from sunup to sundown. When I was not working, I was sleeping. My brother, Jordan, had tried to convince me to start dating again, but I hadn't been ready. Everything with Toni had happened so fast, and my mom wanted to make sure I was not on the rebound from Joi.

My mom was partial when it came to Joi. Joi could do no wrong, and my parents loved her like a family member to this day, and she loved them, too. It was only me and my brother, Jordan, so Joi was the daughter they had never had. They missed her going with them on vacation every summer. Joi and mom would always sneak off and go shopping and sightseeing, followed by more shopping. My dad and I would just stay behind and watch sports. When Joi graduated from law school, my parents canceled their trip to Europe so that they could attend the ceremony.

I was also very close with Joi's mother and father. They were so cool. If there was a concert, play, or some other social event, they were there. Her father was an honorary member of the group Maze. He idolized Frankie Beverly.

He claimed they'd grown up together in the same neighborhood in Philadelphia. If he knew Maze was coming to town, he was the first in line to get tickets for himself, his wife, and anybody else who was interested in going. He made sure he had on his white outfit, white shoes, and definitely the white cap. Joi's mother would be right by his side, singing and dancing to all the same tunes. She was from South Carolina. So when Frankie would start singing "Southern Girl," he would serenade her with the song, and she enjoyed every minute of the attention. Joi and I would just watch them when we would all go to the show together. They were the epitome of old-school love, and it was real.

Whew, all this reminiscing is making me miss Joi more than I should. I know it's going to take some time, but it's difficult, I thought. "Toni, the check-in counter is over here. After we check in, let's go and take a nap before we start walking around the ship," I said.

"No, we are not going to take a nap. You promised me that we could tour this boat, and that is what I would like to do first. We can nap later," Toni complained.

"All right. Chill. It's our honeymoon, so let's try to enjoy it. I only made a suggestion. We can take a mini tour, and then we are going to the cabin. So stop trying to tell me what we are going to do and when you want to do it. I'm a grown-ass man, not a punk. You can make some suggestions, and I can make some suggestions."

"That is not what I was trying to do. I just thought it would make more sense to look around first. Besides, it is going to take them a minute to bring up our luggage."

After we got our key from the check-in desk, we went on a mini tour. Even though I was tired, I didn't want to upset my wife on our honeymoon. I decided to go with the flow.

Wow. I couldn't believe how big this ship was. People were playing miniature golf, climbing rocks, exercising, and swimming. I saw a water park on the main level. There were kids everywhere. I must have seen a plasma TV everywhere I turned. We passed jewelry stores, clothing stores, shoe stores. Toni purchased two straw hats, one for her and one for me. She said that she wanted to be ready when we got to the Bahamas. The nightlife was geared more toward the adults. There were gambling casinos onboard and nightclubs at every end of this ship.

After walking around for about an hour, we finally made it to our suite. As we walked in, I couldn't believe my eyes. This suite was like nothing I had ever seen before. It had a king-size bed with red rose petals spread over the top. I saw a wet bar in the corner, a living room, a dining room, a kitchen, and a Jacuzzi. Royal Caribbean had left a complimentary bottle of champagne on the table. I opened up the bottle of champagne and poured two glasses.

"Let's make a toast," I said.

"To what?" Toni asked.

"To us. May we enjoy everything this cruise has to offer, and I do mean *everything*."

"Baby, we have plenty of time for that. Right now I'm hungry," Toni said.

"Let's order room service."

"Come on, Jay. Stop being such a party pooper."

"A party pooper? I think you got it twisted, because I've been trying to get a party started up in here all day, and all you want to do is leave. It's one excuse after another with you. This is our honeymoon, not some quickie vacation. Just let me know what's up."

"Forget it, Jay. I'll be back when you stop trippin'," Toni snapped.

"So where are you going now?"

"I'm not sure. I need some fresh air."

As Toni left the suite, I had this strange feeling about what had just happened. Here I was feeling guilty about making her feel insecure over Joi, and she seemed to have her own agenda going on.

Am I the one being played now? Something definitely is not right, I thought to myself.

No matter how bad I might want this marriage to work, I just couldn't shake my feelings for Joi, and that was not fair to Toni. I had no right to tell Joi that I wished things had worked out differently. What the hell was I thinking? I could tell that Joi was a little down at my wedding. She was trying her best to put on a good front. Besides everything else, she looked great. Joi had a great fashion sense. She kept up with the latest fashions. Her hair was always in place, and she made sure her manicures and pedicures were well maintained. Joi could make a pair of sweatpants and a T-shirt look good. She just had that look that said: Yes, my game is tight and even if it wasn't, you wouldn't know it.

Mmm, all I keep thinking about is Joi. So how did I get here? I asked myself over and over again.

Finally, the bellman dropped off our luggage. I gave him a ten-dollar tip for his services. He thanked me and immediately left our cabin. I decided to unpack and put my stuff away. I left Toni's luggage over in the corner. I figured that she might have a special way of unpacking her luggage. After I finished, I took a much-needed nap while Toni went to grab a bite to eat.

Two hours later I got up from my nap and noticed that Toni was not back yet. I decided to go and see if I could catch up with her. *She's probably trying to buy out all the stores on this boat,* I thought.

I walked around on the main deck, but I did not see her. I grabbed a slice of pizza and a cold Pepsi and sat near the pool area. It was pretty hot outside, around eighty-eight degrees. People were stretched out on beach chairs, soaking up the sun. Kids were jumping in the pool and having a great time. The water park was crowded, and the lines were long. I didn't know how they managed to have a water park on a ship.

It was time for me to find my wife and put my

feelings for Joi behind me. Even though I was sure that it was easier said than done, I was going to try.

I got back up and went to the upper deck and then the lower deck. I checked the stores, the casino, and a few restaurants, but Toni was nowhere to be found. I was starting to worry, and I went back to the cabin to wait for her.

Another hour and a half went by and still no signs of Toni. Now I was really getting worried, because this was not like her. Just as I got ready to go back out and look for her again, the door handle turned. Toni came in, smiling from ear to ear, with two tiny shopping bags in her hand.

"Hi, Jay. I'm so sorry I took so long, but I just couldn't pull myself away from those stores. You know how I am."

"Toni, you're full of shit. I walked this entire ship, looking for you, and you were nowhere to be found. You sashay your ass all up in here with two little shopping bags, grinning from ear to ear, three and a half hours later, and I'm suppose to be jumping for joy?"

"I told you that I was hungry. So I grabbed a bite to eat at one of the restaurants," Toni explained.

"And I said, 'Let's order room service.' But as usual, you're calling all the shots."

"I needed to get out, Jay."

"Excuse the hell out of me for thinking that my wife wanted to spend some time with her husband on their honeymoon. So, what's really going on with you, Toni?" I snarled.

"Nothing is going on, Jaylen."

"I know I'm not perfect, and I have made some mistakes, but I am trying to make this work. What the hell? We've only been married for two days, and we're already going through this shit. But, hey, if you don't want this, just let me know somethin', because I'm not going to kiss your ass."

Slam!

I left this time and went for a walk. I ended up at the casino. I needed to clear my head and calm down. I walked over to the tables to play some craps. I threw in a one-hundred-dollar bill, and they gave me an equal amount back in casino chips.

"Place your bets," the casino dealer yelled.

I placed my bets and started winning from that point on. I played craps for about forty-five minutes. Afterwards, I cashed in my winnings of $350.00 and went to the dollar slots to see if I could win some more money. I put twenty dollars in the machine, and when I got down to my last three dollars, I hit the five-hundred-dollar jackpot.

I took my winnings and went back to the cabin. Toni was sleeping, with her back facing my direction. I shaved and took a shower. I dialed the extension for room service. I ordered some fresh fruit, omelets, toast, coffee, and juice to be delivered in the morning. I wanted tomorrow to start off on a positive note, because the first day of our honeymoon had been a complete waste of time.

Chapter 3

Infidelity

Joi

"Hello. May I speak to Lex?"

"Hold on," a male voice responded in a soft tone.

"Hello?" Lex whispered.

"Girl! You missed it. The wedding was crazy!" I said.

"For real?" she asked.

"No, Lex, I'm kidding. The wedding almost literally killed me," I said in a sarcastic tone. "What is wrong with you? First, you miss the wedding, and now you are acting like your mind is somewhere else. Is everything okay?"

"I can't talk right now. Call me back or stop by in about an hour," Lex replied.

"Okay," I said.

I hung up the telephone, shaking my head in confusion. Something was not right. My aunt Alexis was always the life of the party—funny, strong, with a heart of gold. She was so pretty. She stood about five feet four and had a brown complexion; pretty, deep, Debbi Morgan–type dimples; shoulder-length hair; and a petite frame. When she laughed, she could light up a room. Lex was thirty-five years old, and I had just celebrated my twenty-ninth birthday.

Lex had the car that always broke down. Hell, her car barely made it two blocks. Just about everywhere we went, either she had a problem with the starter, or she would somehow manage to get a flat tire, with no spare in the trunk. However, she used to be the only one with a ride, so we continued to pile in the front and backseat. I remembered going to the gas station with her, and she would proudly pull up and ask for one dollar's worth of gas. I would just slump down and say to myself, "Oh, no, she didn't . . . Oh, yes, she did." I couldn't believe it. She was too funny. If something was bothering her, she would try not to burden others with her problem, and she would deal with it on her own. She always made light of situations others would have had difficulty dealing with.

I remembered when she found out that she needed to have a kidney transplant because both of her kidneys were not functioning properly; she just went to dialysis and kept it to herself. It was my mom who was all upset and told me that her situation was life threatening. I was so scared that she was going to die, I didn't know what to do. I remembered walking in my backyard, confused and crying, wondering why this was happening. I, like everyone else in the family, wanted to give her a kidney, but I was not a match.

Lex was the baby of the pack. Her mother, who was my grandmother, died when Aunt Alexis was just ten years old. After that, her father and older siblings helped raise her. She always looked out for my cousin Amelia and me. She always told us that we were her favorites. Anyway, to get back to the point, I think just about all our family would have given her a kidney, because she was special to everyone who knew her. Fortunately, my uncle James was a perfect match, and he gave her one of his without a second thought. I just remembered how she would make jokes about growing a mustache because she had her brother's kidney inside of her. We just laughed at her, because it made everything so easy to handle.

Anyway, I went to the store and picked up my dry cleaning and headed on over to Lex's house. The car was not there, so I assumed her husband had taken it somewhere. She had a son from a previous relationship. He was three when she got married.

I hope nothing is wrong with Brandon, I told myself.

I rang the doorbell and no one answered, so I rang it again and knocked on the door.

"Alexis! Open the door, girl," I yelled.

Finally, Lex came to the door, dressed in a robe, drinking tea.

"Are you okay?" I asked.

"Not really."

"What! Do I have to pull it out of you? What is up?"

I could tell she was upset, because it looked like she had been crying. She sipped her tea, and then she looked at me and said, "Do you remember that fat bitch Elisha who works in dietary at the hospital, with Craig?"

"Yeah, I know of her."

"Well, anyway, I found out that he has been having an affair with her triflin' ass behind my back," Lex murmured.

"How did you manage to find this out?" I asked.

"Well, when half your family and friends work at the hospital and everyone is kickin' all these rumors here and there, all I could do was confront him, and he didn't even try to deny it."

"Stop playing. I can't believe he would cheat on you with her. And she got the nerve to work at the local hospital as a dietician, yet she's ironically pulling every bit of three hundred pounds. Something is just wrong with that picture. Her ass must be drinking Slim-Slow. I know I keep going on and on, but I feel like he cheated on me too, and I'm not married to him. And then again, I really don't care what I say about her, because she knew he was married. Well, I hope and pray that you two can work through this, but don't play yourself. You are so much better than that. You might have to go Angela Bassett on his ass and kick him out and sell his shit right in front of these apartments."

"He ain't got shit for me to sell."

"Okay!" I hollered in a sassy tone, snapping my fingers.

"I told him to leave, but he wants to stay and try to work things out. I don't know, Joi. I just don't know," she said, sniffling. "I love him so much, but this is a bit much. I just keep picturing him having sex with her and kissing her big, nasty ass, and then coming home and doing the same thing to me. I am definitely not feeling that."

I gave her a hug and told her if she wanted to go and get a drink or something later on to call me. All of a sudden the door opened, and then it closed. It was him, Craig, Mr. Jackson, with his nasty ass.

Idiot! I thought to myself. I decided to be cordial. I wouldn't let him think she had told me anything. There was no need to make matters worse.

"Hey, Niecy," he said while kissing my forehead.

"Hi, Craig," I replied.

I managed to crack a plastic smile. *Hmm, it's hard keepin' it real and being fake at the same time.*

But I must say, I had on my super-duper plastic smile. Mmm, mmm, mmm, and if he only knew how badly I wanted to charge at his dumb ass, he wouldn't be nowhere near me. *Shit, don't come over here, kissing me on my forehead, after you've been munchin' on your bitch. The last thing I need is y'alls nasty asses on my mind,* I told myself.

"Well, Auntie, I will call you. Peace," I said.

It was really bothering me to see her like this after all she had been through. She had started dating him when he was in the military. He'd come home for a visit, and they'd gone out. He'd proposed to her, and she'd accepted. They seemed to be so in love. He'd been stationed at Fort Hood in Texas, and he would call her just about every night. Lex had been so sprung. It seemed like every night she would play the same old songs over and over again to remind herself of him. All I remembered hearing was the words to "Sukiyaki" by A Taste of Honey or "My First Love," by René & Angela.

She made me feel like the only way I would know that I was in love was if I needed to play those same songs over and over again, as confirmation. They eventually got married on June 13—her birthday. The wedding was very nice, and then Craig flew back to Texas shortly after they were married. The plan was that she would move to Texas with him, but as fate would have it, he received orders to go to Germany. He stayed in Germany for about six months. He had only two weeks left before he would receive an honorable discharge, but he wanted to be with his wife, who was being prepped for a kidney transplant. So he went AWOL, left early, and came home. After a struggle with the military, he was finally awarded a general discharge given the circumstances. Everything seemed to be going so nice and smooth. Now this.

I dialed my aunt's home number.

"Hello?" Lex answered.

"Hey, girl, what's up for tonight? I want to go to The Spot for a drink or two. Do you want to go?"

"What time?" she asked.

"Around tenish," I said.

I only said tenish because I was always late. Everyone kept telling me that I was going to be late to my own funeral. But it didn't matter to my aunt Lex, because her ass was always late, too.

"Let me check with your mother to see if she can baby-sit Brandon. If so, then I will meet you at your mom and dad's house."

I wanted to call the rest of the girls, but I knew my aunt needed me one-on-one tonight. I went home to lie down for a couple of hours. It had been a whole week since Jaylen's wedding, and I was still feeling a little down.

I'm not going to think about it right now, okay! I thought. I had reserved a space to talk about the wedding only once today with my aunt Lex, so I would save my thoughts and feelings for later on at the club. I set the clock for 7:00 p.m.; then I dozed off and woke up at 6:35 p.m. I called my sister to see if she had my diamond stud earrings she'd borrowed a month ago.

"Hey, Gi'ana. I need my earrings tonight," I said.

"What earrings?"

"My diamond stud earrings you borrowed last month."

"Oh? I have to see where I put them. I wore them last weekend to this party, and I can't re-member where I put them, but I know they're here."

"Well, please find them, because I really want to wear them tonight."

"Where you going?" Gi'ana asked.

"Out with Aunt Lex. We're going to stop by The Spot."

"Well, I would go with you guys, but you didn't ask me. It's obvious that I would be imposing."

"That's not true. Aunt Lex needs to talk to me about something," I explained.

"Like what?"

"I have no idea, and even if I did, that would be between us."

"Whatever, Joi."

"Gi'ana, I'll see you later at Mommy's house, with my earrings, okay?"

I loved my sister dearly, but she was just so forgetful. The only reason I could not get mad at her was that she looked exactly like me, just younger, so it was like getting mad at myself. Yet, if it meant cursing myself out, so be it.

Even though there was a seven-year gap between us, I was excited to have a baby sister. She was twenty-two years old and had recently graduated from Hampton University. Her major was early childhood education, and she wanted to be a teacher. It was her passion. She had just passed her Praxis exam and was working on getting a job with the local school district. With all of my sister's education and accomplishments, she was still the annoying younger sister who borrowed things and never gave them back. I swear, if she had lost those earrings somehow, she was replacing them, or else!

I got up, turned on my six-CD-changer stereo. I played my Floetry, Erykah Badu, Anthony Hamilton, Jill Scott, Lalah Hathaway and Will Downing CDs. I just needed to hear something that was soothing and relaxing. Then I jumped in the shower, sang a couple of verses, danced a little, and got out.

Ring . . . ring.

"Hello?"

"Hi," said a male voice.

"Hey, Damon. Can I call you right back? I just got out of the shower, and I'm still drying myself off," I said, then hung up.

I probably should not have told him that, because he stayed so horny. All he wanted to do was get it in. I was not saying that he wasn't all of that, and I was not one to complain about size, but he was just too big. Each and every stroke brought tears to your eyes, and he could care less how you felt just as long as he was satisfied. Afterwards, he just fell asleep, which was a good thing. Sometimes I would just lie there and stare at him, trying to figure him out. This brother was very complex. He just seemed to have issues with rejection. He also had the strangest birthmark on the outside of his left buttock. It was in the shape of Mickey Mouse's face and ears, about the size of a half dollar, and it was two shades lighter than his complexion. I just figured that his parents had visited Disney World a lot when his mother was pregnant with him. It had never really bothered me, and he seemed to care less.

Overall, he was a nice-looking brotha: chocolate, pretty white teeth, six feet two, muscular build, neatly trimmed sideburns, sexy lips, and a deep voice. He had a good job and drove a nice two-seat, black convertible Mercedes Benz, but my mind just wasn't ready for the head games and bullshit that came with it.

Anyway, I could not decide what I wanted to wear, so I stuck to the basics. I figured that if we both were going to be in mourning, why not wear black? I was feelin' my outfit. I had recently lost a few pounds, and the black made me look extra thin. After that, I decided to call Damon back to see what he wanted. The phone rang once and he answered.

"Hello, Damon," I said.

"Hey, baby girl. What's up for tonight?"

"Not much . . . Why?"

"I would like to see you, if at all possible," he said.

For a moment, I figured, what the hell. I had a few hours to burn. But after a session with him, all you wanted to do was sleep.

"Well, I have plans for tonight," I said, hesitating.

"So, I guess I'm not invited."

"It's not like that. Lex and I are going to The Spot to hang out and catch up on some things. I know you don't like going to the club, so I did not bother to ask you."

"Well, I never said I did not like clubs. I just don't like going to them all the time. At some point in your life, it plays out. I just wanted to spend some time with you, but I understand that you have a life too. We can hook up tomorrow, if at all possible."

Damn, this brotha is all up in my space. He needs to get a grip. He didn't even bother to wait a couple of days. If I had told him not tomorrow, he would have said the next day. I should have known this was a possibility, because he had an aggressive personality.

"Look, Damon. I will call you tomorrow and let you know."

"No, call me tonight when you get in . . . please."

He was lucky he said please, because last time I checked, we were not in a monogamous relationship. I went into my living room and poured myself a glass of wine, played my Jill Scott CD, and chilled until 10:00 p.m. Then I grabbed my jacket, keys, and purse, just like the record said, and went to the gas station.

"Please fill me up with regular," I told the attendant.

"Regular?" the attendant asked.

"You damn skippy," I said.

"I'm only asking because I thought that this type of car would get more mileage by using super."

"Heck, no! Gas is too high, and as long as this car gets me from point A to B with regular gas, that is what I will be using." *Simple asses,* I thought.

"That will be twenty-two dollars," he said.

"Thanks."

I then sped off to catch the light on my way to meet Lex at my parents' house. It was 10:30 p.m. and Alexis was nowhere to be found, and she was not answering her phone.

"Mom? Did Lex call you tonight?" I asked.

"Yeah, she said was going to drop Brandon off and meet you here," replied Mom.

I did not want my mom to start asking me any questions, so I just played it off. My mother was a little old-fashioned and a worrywart. She couldn't help it. If I let her, she would drive me crazy. I just knew that she meant well. That was just who she was. But she had a heart of gold, and I wouldn't trade her for anything in the world.

I remembered when I lived at home, she would always wait up for me and then tell me what time I'd got in. I just wished she would relax and understand that I could handle my business in most situations. My father had taught me a lot about having common sense, being street smart, and reading people. I could sum someone up in a flash. However, you could make a mistake and overanalyze.

"So, you never told me about the wedding . . . Daughter," said Mom.

"I'm sorry, Mom. I'll fill you in tomorrow."

"You don't have to if you're not ready."

"Thanks, Mom."

The bottom line was that my aunt Lex needed a cell phone or a BlackBerry. *I'll wait for another fifteen minutes before I call again,* I thought.

"Are you and Lex going to The Spot?" Mom asked.

"Yup!"

"I heard someone got shot there a couple of weeks ago, so be careful," Mom warned.

"I know, Mom, but that happened a block away. Those two guys just happened to be in the club that night, and they were fighting over some girl. Besides, now they have undercover cops there, and everybody is checked before they can enter the club."

"What time will you two be home? Because you know that I worry."

"I don't really know. Around two-ish."

Beep, beep. I peeked out the window, and there was Lex. Brandon was getting out of the car.

"Are you driving?" I yelled outside the door.

"Yup. Hurry up," Lex said.

I kissed Mom and said, "Mom, tell Gi'ana that I'm going to choke her for not bringing over my earrings. She's lucky I brought an extra pair."

I ran out of the house and jumped into Lex's car, and she sped off.

"Who are you running from?" I asked.

"Nobody. I just took the car because if that sorry ass thought he was going to drop me off and take the car to go and see his bitch tonight, he got another think coming, and I don't mean in his pants. He'd better walk, call a cab, or ride his bike."

I said, "I ain't mad at cha."

Finally, we arrived at the club. There were cars everywhere. We had to park in the parking lot of Big Daddy's Fish Market. I wished they were open, because their whiting fish sandwiches were off the hook. No pun intended. As we walked across the street, I thought I saw Damon's black Benz at the corner. I just hoped he didn't start sweating me and trying to follow me home, because I might have to end up staying at my folks' house.

After we went through the long process of getting our pocketbooks and our ID checked thoroughly, we finally paid the cover and went in. We checked our coats and went in search of some seats, preferably at the bar. This was a sure way to get at least one drink out of these cheap men. I found one seat and hurriedly sat in it. I figured I would just stare at the person sitting next to me until he realized we needed two seats and hopefully got up or hit the dance floor. Lex stood there next to me, and we just watched the people dance and enjoy the music. Wow. Some of these females needed to take a second look at their clothes, or the lack thereof, before they stepped out. I was not hatin'; at times, it was just not necessary. Everybody cannot be Halle or J-Lo. Well, at least the DJ was kickin' it.

"This is my song," I said.

I started bopping in my chair, and then someone tapped me on my shoulder and asked me to dance. I said yes and asked Lex to save my seat. He was tall, dark brown, and attractive. He wasn't the best dancer, but he thought so. At one point, he was actually doing the snake.

"What's your name?" he yelled over the music.

"Joi!"

We continued dancing until the song went off. He probably realized that it was useless trying to talk over the music. He thanked me for the dance and walked away. All the cute ones walked away. It was the ugly ones that followed you to your seat, bought you a drink, and asked for your telephone number. You ended up giving them a basic name, like Kim or Lisa, and—it never failed—somebody would come up and call you by your real name. You would think this would piss them off, but noooo, they still hung around and assumed it was either your middle name or nickname.

I went back to my seat and found that Aunt Lex had managed to get another seat at the bar. I sat down and started looking around to see if I knew anyone. I saw a couple of familiar faces but no one I actually socialized with. Either the people were too stuck up or too ghetto.

"Can I get you ladies something to drink?" the bartender asked.

"Yes, I would like a Long Island iced tea, and she would like a Screaming Orgasm," I replied.

"How do you know I want a Screaming Orgasm?"

"Because I'm treating this round, Lexi, and you need one to release all that built-up anxiety. Let it go, girl. Let it go!"

"Excuse you? What about your built-up anxiety or, better yet, wedding day blues?" Lex retorted.

I laughed and placed a twenty-dollar bill on the counter, but the bartender gave it back and told me that someone had already paid for the drinks.

"Excuse me, sir. Who paid for the drinks? So that we can say thank you," I said.

"I'm sorry, miss. He walked away, but if I see him again, I will let you know," replied the bartender.

I was not mad at whoever he was. It was all good. It usually took all night to get someone to buy you water.

"So, Joi, how was the wedding?" Lex asked.

"Girl, it was nice, but still crazy. They are on their honeymoon as we speak. It's too loud in here, so I will tell you everything during the drive home."

"Okay," Lex said.

I looked at my watch. It was almost one in the morning. I couldn't believe how fast time flew when you were having fun.

"Alexis? Is that you?" said a male voice from behind us.

"Yes," said Lex.

"What's up, lady?"

"Hey, Marcus. How's everything with you? Long time, no see," replied Lex.

They exchanged hugs, and then he must have asked her to dance, because she got up and went to the dance floor.

Good for her, I thought.

Aunt Lex was a rare gem. She would give you her last dime, but she didn't take any shit. She was so unpredictable, strong willed, and yet warm. I had always thought of her as my older sister. I called her Auntie Alexis, Lex, or whatever came to mind. She was cool about it because I never disrespected her. She was always there for me. I remember the first time Mother Nature came to visit me. I was fourteen, and I just could not tell my mom. I was hanging out with my aunt Lex at the Laundromat and I just told her. It was 110 degrees outside, and I was miserable. I was experiencing those newly discovered pains called cramps. I made her promise not to tell a soul about what was happening to me, and she never did, I think.

I eventually confided my problem to my closest friend, Faith, and begged her to go and purchase some pads for me and act like they were for her mother. Back in the day, the kids in the neighborhood would tease you if they saw you purchasing feminine products. We walked to the local pharmacy. There was this nice-looking guy who worked the register, and there was no way I was going to let him know I was on my period. Everything was going good until we got up to the register and my friend turned around and announced, "Joi, are these the pads your mother wanted me to get?"

I was so embarrassed that I yelled back, "No, you mean *your* mother!" I could have choked her ass. How dare she put my business out there! Having your period was sacred.

That night I went to Aunt Alexis, crying my eyes out, and told her about my embarrassing day. I lay on her lap, sniffling, while she soothed me and told me there was nothing to be embarrassed about.

"Thank your lucky stars you have it. When there are interruptions with getting it is when you should really panic," she said, laughing. I wouldn't understand what that meant until two years later, when she came home and announced she was pregnant.

"Whew! I'm getting old. I was tired after just one dance," Lex said.

"Why are you wheezing? Do you have asthma, Auntie? Aunt Wheezie?" I laughed.

"No, smart ass, I'm just getting old."

"It's not like you was jamming. All you were doing was swaying to the left and right, clapping your hands," I said, smiling.

"Okay, smart ass."

"So, Lex, are you ready to go?"

"In a minute," she replied.

"Hey, baby girl," a male voice whispered in my ear. I turned around to see who it was.

"Damon? What's up?" I said, sounding suspicious.

"Well, I wanted to check up on you and make sure nobody was up in your face," replied Damon. "That's why I sent you all drinks, so that nobody else would."

"You've been in here all this time? How come you didn't come over sooner?" I asked.

"I wanted to watch you from afar and see how you conduct yourself when I'm not in your presence," Damon informed me.

"What's that supposed to mean?" I said.

"Exactly what I said. I didn't stutter," said Damon.

"Excuse you! I don't have to answer to nobody unless I want to. I appreciate the drinks, but that does not give you the right to secretly watch me all night," I snapped.

"So, can I secretly come over to your place

and watch you all night and morning?" asked Damon.

"No, Damon. Have you been drinking?"

"I hope not, because then you will have to take me home and tuck me in. Friends don't let friends drive drunk, especially friends with benefits," Damon retorted.

"Well, I guess that is why they invented the taxicab. Besides, I'm staying over at my parents' house tonight," I said.

"Damn, is it like that?" he said.

"It's just like that," I replied.

I was ready to go now. All I needed to do was find Aunt Lex. For some reason, I no longer felt comfortable. She came back, and I told her what had happened.

"Girl, he might be a modern-day stalker," she said, laughing.

I told her to stop playing. We grabbed our pocketbooks and headed for the door. On my way out, I saw Damon all up in some female's face. I suddenly felt a sense of relief come over me, but then I noticed him looking at me leave while he was still in this girl's face. He seemed to abruptly end the conversation as I got closer to the door. I whispered to Lex that Damon was in pursuit. No sooner than we hit the door, we walked quickly to the car, and Lex drove off before I could even close my door.

"Are you okay, Joi? Next time please give a sista a little warning."

"Yeah, I might just be acting a tad paranoid

because I had that drink tonight. I told Damon that I was staying at my parents' house."

"What did he say?" asked Lex.

"What could he say? He is not the boss of me."

"Well, I'm staying the night, too. I don't feel like going home."

"Are you going to call your husband and tell him where you're at?"

"You've got to be kidding. I can't even stand to look him in the face right now. Every time I think about him and his fat bitch . . . I can't even go there now."

Lex pulled up in front of my parents' house. We looked around for Damon's car for about a minute and quickly crept inside. Once inside, we both breathed a sigh of relief. Lex went to check on Brandon, and I dozed off on the couch.

Chapter 4

Blind Date

Faith

I picked up the telephone to call Joi, and I apparently dialed the wrong number. A man answered the phone.

"Hello," he said in a groggy and heavy voice. He seemed to be a little annoyed that I had woken him up.

"I'm sorry. I must have dialed the wrong number."

"Naw, it's cool. What number did you mean to dial?"

"I meant to dial five-five-five-one-two-one-three."

"Well, this number ends in one-two-three-one."

I had inadvertently switched around the last two digits. He started to laugh. He told me that this number belonged to his mother, and he had stopped by to visit and had dozed off before I had called.

"Well, at least you have a sense of humor. Most people would have hung up on me," I said.

"Well, maybe I'm not most people, and maybe I like the sound of your voice."

"Oh really?" I said, sounding pleasantly surprised. "Actually, I hate my voice. It's so mundane. It just lacks excitement."

"So, Miss I Hate My Voice, may I ask your name?"

"Faith. And yours, Mr. I Fell Asleep at My Mother's House?"

"Okay, you got me on that one. That was cute, real cute."

From that point on, the conversation just fell into place. He told me that his name was Tyree, and that he was originally from Syracuse, New York, and had moved to New Jersey while in the military.

"So, Tyree, are you married or single?"

"I'm divorced, with no kids. What about yourself?" he asked in return.

"Most definitely single and looking. I also do not have any kids."

We continued talking for about another hour or so. The time was flying by so quickly. The conversation was on point, and I knew I didn't want to hang up.

"So, Faith, when can I meet you in person?" Tyree asked.

"So soon?" I asked.

"Well, the sooner the better. I mean, we are consenting adults. No need to play games. Right?"

"It's not that at all. It's just that I just met you over the telephone, and, you know, people are crazy."

"Oh, now I'm crazy? For all I know, you could be nutty as hell, but I'm willing to take that chance," he said.

"Look, we can go back and forth. The bottom line is I'll check my schedule and get back to you."

"Well, since you put it like that, I guess I'll just have to wait," he said.

He retrieved my number from the caller ID and asked me if he could call me later that night. I told him that he could call me. He then gave me his home phone number. He sounded a little thugged out, which was usually not my preference, but I thought to myself, *What the hell.* Sometimes a little thug could be sexy. He definitely had my attention. I was lonely and would talk to the mailman if he gave me the time between deliveries. I definitely was going to call Mr. Tyree. I figured he was from Syracuse, and he might know how to keep me warm at night when it was cold.

Oh no. I was supposed to go to church with Tina tonight. She lived next door to me, and I'd known her for a while. I couldn't keep canceling on her. I would just call her and make up something. Besides, I was really tired, and I just wanted to lie down and relax. Tina was a Christian. She was married and had four children and one on the way. She lived a comfortable and conservative lifestyle. She meant well, so I would try to listen and do things with her. She felt that my life would be a lot more fulfilling if I went to church and developed a closer relationship with the Lord. She probably was right, but I knew that I was not disciplined enough for that type of lifestyle. Tina understood because she had hung out at the clubs with Joi, Taj, Eboni, and me in the past. She had finally turned her life around, and I was so happy for her. I most definitely believed in God, and I did go to church every now and then. Believe me, I prayed about it, because I thought about my salvation often.

I knew that I had issues, no doubt. Tina had never overstepped her boundaries. We had a mutual respect for each other. Anyway, I dialed her number and waited for her to pick up. Maybe her machine would come on, and I could leave a message after I listened to an entire collection of gospel favorites.

Click, click.

"Hello?" said a female voice.

"Oh, hi, Tina. This is Faith, and I . . . uh . . . have cramps and won't be able to go to church with you tonight. Please don't be mad."

"I'm not mad, Faith. If you do not feel well, that's understandable," said Tina. "Take some Advil or Excedrin, and get some rest. We'll get together another time. Let me know if you need anything. God bless you."

After she hung up, I felt so bad. It was like she already knew, but she understood me enough to allow me my space and not pressure me. I guess she figured when the time was right, it would be right. It was all good.

I climbed into bed around 8:00 p.m. and turned on my television. Then I called the number Tyree had given me and his machine came on. "Hello. This is Tyree. You know what to do. Peace." I left a message "Tyree, this is Faith. Give me a call. I'll be up for a while."

I could tell by the options on the telephone that he had given me a cell phone number. "To leave a voice message, press one or just wait for the tone. To send a numeric page, press two now. At the tone, please record your message." That was definitely a sign. *What's up on the home front that he forgot to tell me?* I wondered. I lay there watching the clock every five minutes. Before long it was 9:00 p.m. *Where is he? Who is he with? Here we go again,* I thought. *Ring.* I looked at my caller ID and saw that the number was restricted. He must have hit *67. *Doesn't he know that game recognizes game?*

"Hello?" I said softly, wanting to sound sleepy and not like I was waiting up for his call, even though I was.

"Hey, baby. Did I wake you up?"

"No, I was just lying down, watching TV," I murmured.

"Were you thinking about me?" he asked.

"Yes, I was. So did you go out tonight?" I queried.

"Nah! I was just chilling with my boys."

"Oh, I thought you were out with your girl-friend." There was silence. "Why are you so quiet all of a sudden?"

"I'm not quiet. I was just a little shocked by the statement," he admitted.

"I'm not trying to be all up in your business. It was meant to be a joke. But since we are now on that subject, I would like to know these things up front."

"Yeah, man, whatever," he said, with a slight attitude.

"Excuse you?" I replied.

"It's just an expression, and what's up with all the questions?"

"I just want to know what I'm getting into," I said.

"Well, if you give me the opportunity to have a decent conversation with you, you will know everything you need to know. First of all, I just met you. I thought we made a connection. The last time I checked, I've never physically spent any time with you, and yet you're tripping on me like we're in this heavy relationship, and I just met you over the telephone today. Yo, chill."

"You're right. I apologize. My bad. Please forgive me. I just want you to be straight up with me, no matter how much you may think it will hurt me. I can respect a man who can be straight up."

"That's what's up. So when can we meet in person? I have some spare time tomorrow. We can hook up and go to a movie or dinner," he said.

"I'd like that. We can meet tomorrow at six o'clock at the Home Depot. I have to pick up some stuff, and I could use a man's assistance. Are you feeling me?" I asked, smiling.

"That will work. I hope you are as pretty in person as you sound on the phone. You know, for some reason, I enjoy talking to you. I'm not a phone person, and I'm tired from working out all morning and chillin' with my boys tonight. But your voice is so sexy. Normally, people in general would annoy me by asking me a whole lot of questions about what's going on in my life."

"That was a sweet thing to say. I'm trippin'," I told him. "I just felt like I've known you for so much longer than I actually have. It's so hard meeting somebody nowadays. I think I'm a pretty together sister. I'm cultured, educated, single, and independent with no children. I might not be Beyoncé or J-Lo, but I consider myself well put together, very attractive inside and out."

"And that's a good thing, because I like women with confidence."

"Well, I'm strong on so many levels," I assured him.

"Not to change the subject, but what are you wearing?" he asked.

"Why?"

"'Cause! I'm feelin' you, and I might need to see you tonight."

"I don't think I said anything to you to turn you on, or anybody else for that matter."

"So, you never answered my question. What are you wearing?"

I couldn't believe he was turning the tables on me and being so straightforward. But a real woman would just handle her business and work that phone sex. Between you, these walls, and me, I was wearing some flannel pajamas, a head scarf, and bunny slippers, but he didn't need to know that. Now I needed to turn on my fantasy phone line switch.

"I'm wearing some black thigh highs with a matching garter belt, matching bra, and a thong. If you want to know what I'm doing, I'm just lying here, listening to slow music on the radio, thinking about you."

"Damn, girl, don't start anything you can't finish. Can I come over right now?" he asked.

"Not tonight. As much as I'm enjoying this conversation, I can wait until tomorrow."

The truth of the matter was that I did not have on any of that shit, and I would be damned if I was going to jump up and run to the mall and purchase a hundred dollars' worth of Victoria's Secret lingerie. I needed to see what this brotha looked like first. I might need to go to Wal-Mart or Kmart and grab a five-dollar nightie. However, I could not believe the effect this man was having on me. Was it because I just needed some, or what? I mean, I wanted to eventually settle down and get married and have some children.

"Well, Tyree, I look forward to meeting you tomorrow. Don't forget. I'll be at the Home Depot off of Arcadia Highway at six o'clock, sitting in a black Ford Expedition. Don't tell me about your vehicle or what you look like. Just surprise me. Well, I'm a little tired, so I'm going to hang up and get some sleep."

"I can't wait to meet you," he said just before he hung up.

Within seconds, I dozed off. The next morning I overslept because I had forgotten to set my alarm clock. Who cared? It was Saturday, and I had a date, a blind date. Suddenly, I started feeling a little weary. Relationships just didn't seem to work out for me, and here I was, getting all excited, and it might not work out. I had to stop being so negative. From this point on, I was going to be positive, and everything would be all right. If it was meant to be, it would be.

What I needed to do was go to the grocery store. My refrigerator was so bare. I just hated to shop. The people were crazy in the parking lot, and food was so expensive. Back in the day, before food stamps became credit cards, I used to buy food stamps from my cousin Nay Nay. She would sell me one hundred dollars' worth for fifty dollars. I knew she had kids, so I made sure she went shopping with me most of the time. She was a good mom to her kids. She just needed some extra cash to cover some other expenses, and if I didn't buy the food stamps, she would sell them to somebody else. I just hated to shop with them, because the check-out clerks would go out of their way to embarrass you. They treated you real nice until you started struggling to rip out those food stamps. And—just my luck—there would be a nice-looking brotha standing behind me, waiting to check out.

I remembered one time this happened to me, and there was no way I was going to let him see those food stamps. I forgot about keeping it real. I held up the line, ran to my car, grabbed my American Express card, and paid fifty dollars for my groceries. He just smiled and paid me no further attention. I had another unsavory incident with food stamps when the cashier needed to give me back some change. The cashier made it a point to start yelling stupid shit, like "I need change for a five-dollar food stamp in aisle two." Sometimes you just wanted to say, "Heffa, walk your lazy ass over to customer service and get change so you can stop putting my business all out in the store." The words just dragged on, and it seemed like everybody was staring at me. I just wanted to slap the cashier right in the face. Eventually, I got my food and left.

Whew! I needed to calm my nerves. I put on one of my favorite radio stations, WZJP 105.5. I couldn't commit, because I liked them all. I switched channels left and right until I found what I was looking for. In the morning, I liked to listen to all the crazy radio personalities. I switched to one of the stations, and the DJ was playing "Float On." This particular station loved playing old-school records. The problem was not the radio station, but the song's lyrics. They knew they needed to change those words. Believe me, my version would be a little different.

I pulled up to my apartment complex and made my way up the stairs, with my bags. Once inside, I put the groceries away and straightened up the place. It wasn't really dirty, just a little dusty here and there. I got my own place only about six months ago. Before that, I was living at home for a minute. I had finally gotten a job as a certified nursing assistant at the local hospital. I worked three days a week, with twelve-hour shifts, and on alternating weekends. I am currently attending nursing school because I want to help people. After all I have gone through so far to become a nurse, I should have studied to become a doctor. But I am content. Nowadays, just about everyone looked like doctors and nurses. Everyone in the hospital wore scrubs, and they looked nice with the clog sandals and sneakers. A couple of times, I wore my uniform to happy hour.

Now, I needed to get my nails and feet done. I needed to look my best without him recognizing my true effort. It was three o'clock, so they needed to get me in and out. I drove up to Forty-second St. Nails, which was owned by my girl Lynn. The parking lot was almost empty, but when I stepped inside, all the stations were full.

"Ba thao son," she said to an older man sitting behind the register. Basically, she told him to take off my old polish. He came over to me and signaled for me to follow him. I spotted my girl Taj sitting at the pedicure station. I signaled her to call me in two hours. I was seated at station eight. It was obvious the older man did not speak English. He grabbed my hands and started removing my nail polish. Time flew when you were treating yourself. After my manicure, pedicure, and massage, I noticed that two hours had passed. I tipped everyone and ran out the door. I still had to get ready for my date with my mystery man.

I drove home and found my answering machine blinking. *Beep.* "Hey, babe, this is Tyree. Give me a call. I need directions to this Home Depot."

Yes! He didn't cancel, because I would have been pissed off. It was 4:45 p.m., and I needed to start getting ready. I figured that I would wear a pair of jeans with a matching jacket. I wanted to look cute and casual, but not anxious. I took a bath, put lotion all over my body, and sprayed on some Dream Angels perfume by Victoria's Secret. I didn't have to do my hair, because it was already done. While I was brushing my teeth, the phone rang again. I had to run and answer it with a mouth full of toothpaste.

"Hewow? Dis is her. Wold on peez." I went into the bathroom and rinsed out my mouth. "Hi, Tyree! Yes, I'm ready."

"Do you have the directions?" he asked.

"Yes, I do." I gave him the directions to the Home Depot.

"Okay. I'll see you there shortly," he replied, then hung up.

"Dammit. Where are my car keys?" I yelled. I started panicking because I wanted to get there before him so I could get a good look first. I finally found them in the usual spot—my pocketbook. *I must be trippin'*. I jumped on the freeway, and within ten to fifteen minutes, I was in the Home Depot parking lot. I drove up and parked close to the front entrance, and then I pulled down my mirror to make sure I was straight. I was so nervous. I didn't know what to do. I turned on my CD player to calm myself down. I saw a white SUV pull into the parking lot. The vehicle was moving very slowly. I could tell the driver was looking for something more than a parking space. Tyree knew the model of my car, even the color. He must have recognized that it was me, because he pulled up right next to me. We both smiled, and I turned my head as if I was shy. He stepped out of his truck, wearing a black Sean John sweat suit, bright white Nikes, designer shades, and a knit cap. Mmm, he was looking good.

"Faith?" he asked.

"Yes!" I said, smiling anxiously.

"I'm Tyree. I just wanted to make sure I had the right person before I gave you a hug."

"Well, what are you waiting for?" I asked.

He came over to me and hugged me so tight, and I wanted to melt. Let me tell you, this brotha was all of that. I didn't know what cologne he was wearing, but it smelled so good on him. He was attractive, and he definitely worked out. His arms were nice and strong. When he hugged me, I wanted to kiss him. I could tell he was a little thugged out, which was turning me on even more.

Forget Home Depot. I'd rather take him to my home, I thought to myself.

Before we went into the store, we sat in my car and talked for a minute.

"So, Faith, are you hungry? I know you need to get something at Home Depot, but we can grab something to eat. I can drive, and we can leave your car here."

"Leave my car here?" I said.

"Yes, here in the parking lot. We'll be back before they close. I promise. But, if you feel that strongly about it, we can take your car and leave mine here. Whatever."

"Okay. We can go in my car, and I can get what I need when we get back."

"That's what's up," he said.

"So, where would you like to go, Tyree?" I asked.

"Well, I don't eat red meat or pork, so we can go to Olive Garden," he suggested.

I couldn't help but imagine having dinner with him. My mind was playing games. It took me about fifteen minutes to get to the restaurant, but hey, he was treating, so I did not complain. The parking lot was a little bare, which was good. I hoped it meant the service would be fast without sacrificing the taste of the food. He opened the door to the restaurant for me, and we walked in. The hostess asked how many were in our party and if we wanted smoking or non-smoking. He told her, "Two for nonsmoking."

Mmm, a take-charge gentleman with a little thug attitude. Now that's what I'm talking about. I felt so safe with him already. He was turning me on. *Hmm, forget Olive Garden!* I thought to myself. He stood about six feet five and had a medium brown complexion, muscular arms and chest, and a bald head. He was definitely into clothes, because he had mad style. I really did not have a preference with regard to complexion. I could care less whether you were light-skinned or dark-skinned, just as long as you had it going on to me. That was all that really mattered.

"Your table is ready," the hostess said. Tyree grabbed my hand and gently led me to the table.

"Can I sit next to you?" he asked.

"I don't see why not," I replied.

Tyree was so close to my ear, I almost passed out. He ordered me a glass of merlot and a Heineken for himself.

"So, do you like what you see? Because I definitely like what *I* see," he said.

I almost choked on my water. It had been too long since I'd had a man for him to be all up in my face. "I'm very pleased. I've heard horror stories about blind dates."

"Oh? I'm your first?" he asked.

"No, my second, but I'd rather not talk about it."

"So, I guess yours is one of those horror stories you just mentioned?"

"Yes, it was," I said, laughing. I just shook my head. If only he knew.

One time, my girlfriend Bre' showed my picture to her boyfriend Rick's friend Rasheed, and he wanted to meet me. Well, we talked a couple of times on the phone. Rasheed's conversation was a little whacked, but he was sweating me so bad to meet up in person, I just figured why not. He acted as though he had fallen in love with me over the phone, telling me shit, like "It seems as though I've known you all my life." I asked Bre' what he looked like. All she said was he was cool, rapped, played sports (of course, nothing major), and was dark skinned, with braids in his hair.

I should have known her taste would be off, since her man looked tricked up. He was ex-

tremely unattractive. His head was huge, and
his hairline started behind his ears. His vo-
cabulary was shot, and all he wore was baggy
clothes with last year's fucked-up dreads. She
was a cute girl, and all she wanted to do was
use him because he sold drugs and drove
around in a Range Rover. She was shallow and
confused, but she was still my girl. She just
knew I was lonely, so her heart was in the right
place. Anyway, he asked me to come to his
house because his car had broken down. I
agreed. So I drove to his house, which happened to be his *parents'* house, and I saw this
fake-looking Rastafarian with a hoodie walking
down the steps.

Please don't let this be him. Please . . . , I thought.

It *was* him, and I couldn't believe it. His lips
were huge! He would never get the opportunity
to kiss me in his dreams. Oh hell no! I was going
to put my foot up Bre's ass for about a week. To
make a long story short, we talked for about fifteen minutes, and then he asked me if I wanted
to get something to eat. Of course, I told him
that I had already eaten. He kept telling me
how pretty I was every five minutes, and that he
knew he was out of my league. What was I supposed to say? "You got that shit right . . . You're
not my type. I can't believe I'm stuck in this car
with you, and I have to figure out a way to
escape."

Luckily, his mother called out to him that he
had a phone call. He asked me to wait a

minute and said that he would be right back. I immediately called my girl and told her to call me in ten minutes and make up anything so that I would have to leave right away. He came back and asked me how I felt now that I had met him.

"Well, I think you're a nice person, but I'm not looking for a relationship right now." I didn't think that was what he wanted to hear, but too bad. He then asked me for a hug, and I agreed. I really felt bad because he was such a nice loser, just not for me. My girl Shay rang my phone in exactly ten minutes and two seconds.

"Hey, girl. Where are you at?" asked Shay.

"I'm out on a date with my friend. Why?" I said. I made sure he heard that.

"Well, damn, bitch. You act like you enjoying yourself!" she said, crackin' up laughing.

"What do you mean, he never picked you up from work? Girl, I'm busy. You can't get anybody else to pick you up? Girl, you always need me for some bullshit. If he can leave you hanging at your job in the dark, you need to get rid of his ass."

"Heffa, don't get it twisted, because you know I have my own car and don't need shit from nobody. Just get your ass out of there," she said.

"All right, already. Give me about twenty to thirty minutes. I'll be there."

I told him I had to leave, and he said he understood. He asked if he could have a kiss. I told him that I didn't get down like that on the first date and that I was only looking for a friendship—nothing intimate. He said he would call me later to make sure I got home safe. I thanked him and drove off. He called me about one hundred more times. After call 101, he finally got the message.

However, tonight was different. I had butterflies in my stomach, and my mind kept wandering off. I imagined us making love, with his body pressed against mine, with him kissing me all over, holding me all night.

"Woooo," I said.

"Are you all right?" Tyree asked.

"Yeah, I'm just thinking about something."

"Thinking about what?" he asked.

"It's personal."

"Okay."

We both ordered the grilled chicken with angel-hair pasta in a fettuccine alfredo sauce. The restaurant was as empty as the parking lot. We sat off in the corner in a secluded area. I could not believe that I was actually on a date with Tyree. I tried to eat cute, but the way he was throwing down, I just started eating like my normal self. After we ate dinner and drank a little, he paid the bill and we left.

"Home Depot closes in about an hour. Are you ready to go back now and get your car?" I asked.

"Yeah, we can do that. Do you need me to stop in afterwards and tuck you in?" he asked.

"No, not tonight. I'm a little tired. Maybe another time."

"That's cool," he replied.

I drove back to Home Depot. We went inside and picked up some items for my place. As we left the store, he held my hand again and led me to his car. He claimed he wanted me to see his truck. I looked in the front seat, and he opened the back door. He had everything in this truck.

"What is this? A truck or a Winnebago?" I asked.

"Why do you ask that?"

"Because you have everything in here."

Before I knew it, he kissed me on my lips, and I kissed him back as we stood outside of his truck. The kiss lasted for about five minutes straight. I couldn't believe it. The kiss was everything I had hoped it would be. I could tell he wanted it to go further, but I wasn't exactly ready for that. We hugged and stared at each other briefly. The butterflies inside of me were out of control, and when he hugged me again, all I could feel were hard muscles everywhere, and I mean *everywhere*. I had to exercise extreme control. I gently pulled myself away.

"Good night, Tyree. I had a great time tonight," I said softly.

"I had a great time, too, and I look forward to seeing you again," he said.

"I'd like that."

"Please call me when you get home so that I know you're okay."

"I will," I promised.

We both pulled off at the same time. He went in one direction, and I went in another.

The date had been nice, and I felt comfortable. I knew this was who I wanted to get to know better. When we did get to that point of intimacy, which hopefully would be soon, I wanted it to be special.

He called me when he pulled into his driveway. I didn't even get a chance to call him, like he had asked me to do.

"So, what are you doing?" he asked.

"I'm getting ready to take a cold shower," I joked.

"I wish I could take one with you."

"One day soon, real soon. Uh, Tyree can you call me back in about fifteen minutes, when you get settled in?"

"All right."

"Hey, Tyree, I love you, and thanks for everything tonight."

I had no idea what had come over me, but I had actually used the *L* word. It was official; I had issues. I couldn't even take it back, and I was not even sure that I wanted to.

"I love you, too, boo. I'll call you back in a few, okay?"

Okay. Mmm, he called me boo. That is so cute, I thought.

We hung up, and I jumped in the shower. I

was on cloud nine. I was falling in love, and there wasn't a damn thing I could do about it. Then again, maybe it was just lust, but who cared. It felt too good for me to worry about it now.

Ten minutes later I got out of the shower and dried myself off. I must say, I still had it going on with my figure. I still had to work out and eat right on a regular basis. I refused to let myself go. I worked out three times a week at the gym.

I waited and waited for his call. I figured he had just dozed off. I called him back and left a message on his voice mail. I should have gotten his home phone number. All of a sudden, I got this insecure feeling that there was someone else in his life. I never got a straight answer. I grabbed my pillow and turned on the television. I watched everything there was to watch for the next two and a half hours. He never called me back.

I'd been overprotective of him, especially when it came to his female acquaintances. Gi'ana had only been seven years old at the time of Wil's death, and the only thing she'd been protective of was her toys.

In high school, Wil was voted most popular and most attractive. He stood about six feet seven inches tall, and he looked like the actor and basketball player Rick Fox. He had so many girls chasing after him, my mother put a block on the telephone. There was one girl that he seemed to like a lot more than the others. Her name was Vanessa. She looked like the R & B singer Tamia. Her parents were strict, but they did allow her to go to the prom with Wil. I didn't know what happened to their relationship. It just seemed to fizzle.

Wil was so good at basketball that the NBA was ready to draft him straight out of high school. However, my parents were not comfortable with him not attending college first. My father would say, "Son, basketball can wait, but your education can't." My mother would just agree with my father, because she wasn't ready to deal with Wil being in that lifestyle so young. Wil finally went off to college to play basketball in Florida. During the basketball season, he played above and beyond what the coaches and scouts had expected. He had so many groupies, and he was only a freshman. He eventually met this young lady named Kendal. I could tell she was his type. She was cute. She had brown skin and dimples, and her hair was down her back. Kendal obviously loved throwing her hair up into a ponytail, because that was how I remembered seeing it most of the time.

They dated for almost four months, and things seemed to be going great until one day Wil came home for spring break with a bruise over his left eye. My mother and father asked him what had happened, but he just shrugged it off and said that someone had accidentally elbowed him in a game of basketball. He seemed troubled, but I did not want to ask him any questions. Another time he came home, I could hear him arguing with Kendal on the telephone. He was yelling, and I remembered him asking her, "Well, Kendal, if you're not dealing with this asshole, why does he seem to have a beef with me?" He looked up and saw me listening from the window and abruptly ended the call. I knew that something was seriously wrong now. I knew now that that bruise had come from a fight, and it had something to do with Kendal. I waited in my room for a little over an hour. I eventually went and knocked on Wil's bedroom door.

"Come in," he said.

"Hey, Wil. Is everything okay?" I asked.

"What do you mean, is everything okay? Of course, everything is okay. Why do you ask, Joi?"

"Well, because I heard you yelling on the telephone, and you never yell."

"Come here, girl. I'm cool, and you do not have to worry your pretty little self about me. I just have to take care of some things, and then I'll be good," he said.

"Are you sure? Because if it has something to do with Kendal, I'll kick her butt. I know I'm only fourteen years old, but I will fight her if she makes my brother mad."

Wil just laughed, and that made me feel better. He would take me to McDonald's or to Burger King and treat me to lunch. I soon forgot about the whole incident. My dad and Wil spent a lot of time together. They were so close, and they shared a special bond. They would sit outside on the porch for hours, talking and laughing. Wil was also an honorary member of Maze, and he would go off to the concerts with my mom and dad. Mom would do all his laundry when he came home from school and would make his favorite dinner.

After about two weeks of being home, Wil returned to college in Florida to finish up his spring semester. My parents drove him to the airport to catch his flight. Mom did not cry as much as before, because she knew he would be coming home for the summer. She kissed his cheek and told him that she was so proud of him. Dad gave him a hug and a pat on the back. Gi'ana and I held on to his shirt. Wil picked Gi'ana up and gave her a big kiss and hug. He told her that he was going to bring her back a doll for her to play with. He bent down and gave me a big hug and kiss also. Wil told me to hang in there and that he would be back home before I knew it. We watched as his plane took off into the sky. Gi'ana and I tried to wave to the plane, but eventually, it disappeared into the clouds.

"Bye, Wil. Call me later," I said.

"Me too," Gi'ana yelled.

On the way home from airport, my mother started to cry. "I just hate it when he has to leave. I wish his college wasn't so far away."

"He'll be home in May, Mom, so don't cry." I said.

My dad decided to stop for some ice cream at the custard stand. He was sad, and he needed to create a distraction so we could all cheer up. We got out of the car and ordered whatever we wanted. After that, we went home.

One month later . . .

Everything was going fine. The weather was getting warmer and school would be out soon and I couldn't wait. I was coming inside the house after playing with my friends when the telephone rang. My mother walked over to answer it.

"Wil shot? Who shot who?" Mom yelled in a frantic voice. "Please don't tell me that my baby is dead! Please don't say that!"

My father rushed over and took the phone from her as he tried to make sense of what the call was about. My aunt and uncle were visiting at the time, and they rushed into the room to comfort my mother. I could see the fear in my father's eyes, but he didn't break down, because he knew he had to be strong for all of us. My mom was screaming, and my dad punched the wall so hard, I thought the house was going to fall apart.

"I have to go down to Florida. I have to go to Florida right now to check on my boy," Dad said.

He grabbed his jacket and his keys, and my mom rushed to the door. "Wait for me please. I need to go with you," she said.

She turned around to ask my aunt and uncle if they could watch over my little sister, Gi'ana, and me until they returned. I was so scared to ask what had happened. I just knew it was something really bad, and as bad as I wanted to know, I really didn't want to.

It was clear that my aunt and uncle were nervous and upset, but they were trying their best to put up a front.

"Aunt Linda, can I call my mom?" I asked.

"Uh, let me try to reach her first, and then I will pass you the phone, Joi," she hesitantly replied.

"All right," I mumbled.

I watched my aunt Linda dial a number on the telephone. She walked in the other room and started whispering. All of a sudden I heard a slight gasp. She put the telephone down and walked outside. My uncle Ray followed her. I saw him grab her and hug her real tight. Now,

I was confused, and I wanted to find out what was going on.

"Aunt Linda, was that my mom on the telephone?" I yelled through the screen door.

"Oh yes, baby. She said she was at the gas station and would call you back in a few."

"Where was my father?" I quizzed.

"Oh, uh, he was pumping the gas I think," said Aunt Linda.

It was obvious they were keeping something from me. My uncle lit up a cigarette on the front step. I headed outside to find out what was going on.

"What are you guys keeping from me? Where is Wil? Is he okay? I heard Mom say something about getting shot," I said.

There was dead silence for about five seconds, and I felt this strange sensation in my stomach.

"Where did my mom and dad go, and what happened?" I yelled.

"Sweetheart, calm down. Everything is going to be just fine," Uncle Ray said in a sad tone.

"Just tell me what happened," I persisted. "It is so obvious that you two are upset. Where is the telephone? I'll call my mom and dad myself."

"Honey, please come and sit down on the step. Wil was hurt, and your mom and dad went to check on him," Uncle Ray explained.

"Hurt how?" I cried.

"I'm not exactly sure. That is what we are waiting to hear from your mom and dad," said Uncle Ray.

The next several hours felt like days. I couldn't fall asleep, because I just kept thinking something really bad had happened to my brother.

"Dear Lord, I know you love me and my family. I just need to ask you to make sure Wil is okay. I'm scared that something very bad has happened, and I don't know what to do. Please Lord, take care of my brother, because I love him so much and he makes me laugh. He is the best big brother a sister can have. Please Lord. Amen."

I finally fell off to sleep. I woke up the next morning and immediately went to my parents' room. They still were not home. My aunt and uncle kept telling me that they were going to call later. The day came and went. There was emptiness in the house, but I couldn't figure it all out. I finally dozed off again.

The next morning I jumped up and ran into my parents' room. This time my mom was sitting on the bed, wiping her face. Her eyes were puffy, and she looked like she had not slept for weeks.

"Mom, what's the matter?" I cried.

She grabbed my hand and looked up at me with a weak smile and tearful eyes. "It's your brother, Wil. He was hurt real bad, baby," she said in a scratchy, low tone.

"Where is he, Mommy? Where is Wil?" I cried.

"Wil is in Heaven, sweetheart."

"What do you mean, he's in Heaven? He just went to Florida."

"Joi, Wil is dead."

At that moment, everything in me just fell apart. I thought this was just one big, ugly dream. I refused to believe it. I ran to my room and grabbed the telephone so that I could call Wil's phone.

Ring . . . ring.

"Hi, this is Wil. I can't take your call right now, but leave me your name and number and I'll call you back later. Peace."

"Wil, this is your sister Joi. I need for you to call me at home as soon as you get this message please. Please, Wil. I need to ask you something, so please, please call me. It's important. I love you," I said in a hysterical voice.

I turned around, and my mom was coming toward me to comfort me.

"Joi, please calm down."

"No, I have to wait for Wil to call me back. I told him it was important. So I'm just going stand here and wait."

"Baby, Wil is gone. He's not coming back, and he's not going to call."

"Liar. Don't say that. You hear me. Don't say that ever again, Mom. He is coming back home. So just shut up and mind your own business, because you don't know what you're talking about. I just left him a message."

At that point, my dad ran upstairs to see what was going on. He could tell I had just gotten the news, and he just grabbed me and held me tight. I cried for what seemed an eternity.

The next several days were filled with making

funeral arrangements and notifying our family
and friends. The local newspaper was running
an article about Wil daily. The headlines were
saying: BASKETBALL STAR FATALLY WOUNDED,
GUNMAN CLAIMED SELF DEFENSE. There was so
much drama going on, I couldn't think straight.
My parents made sure Wil had the best final
resting gear. Although he owned a lot of suits,
my dad went out and purchased another one,
along with a new shirt, a tie, and shoes. The
local barber cut his hair. My parents spared
no expense under the circumstances, and so
many people came to pay their last respects. My
grandparents drove up from South Carolina. Wil's teammates and coach flew in from
Florida. They signed a basketball in his honor
and placed it in his casket. I saw people he'd
hung out with in high school and a few ex-
girlfriends. One ex-girlfriend in particular,
Vanessa, was taking it extremely hard. It was obvious how much he meant to her. She never
stopped crying throughout the entire service.
She had been his girlfriend during his senior
year in high school. He had taken her to the
prom. The deaconess in the church had to
check on her quite often. The reporters were
outside having a field day. There were so many
people in attendance that the local police department had to come and direct traffic.

The funeral was sad. The service lasted for
about two hours. Each and every last one of his
teammates spoke about Wil. Some of them

made us laugh, and some made us cry. His high school and college coaches spoke briefly. They were too choked up to finish. The church choir sang two really nice songs. They had so many people on their feet. They were praising Jesus, shouting, crying. My mom was pretty strong throughout the funeral, but when they went to close the casket, she lost her composure.

"Don't you close that casket. I'm not done yet. I need to see my baby," she cried.

Right away, my dad grabbed her and hugged her. He was trying to be strong, but I saw the tears streaming down his face.

"Don't let them take my baby," Mom cried.

"It's going to be all right. He's in a better place," my dad soothed.

"Why? Oh, why did he kill my boy?" Mom asked.

I ran up to my mother and told her that I would take care of her. She hugged me, and it seemed to comfort us both. A young girl from the church started singing "His Eye Is on the Sparrow."

At this point, it seemed as though everybody was in tears. I looked around and saw so many wet faces. Wil's teammates served as the pall-bearers. Just as they were about to take his casket out, his girlfriend, Kendal, walked up and fainted at the casket. Her mother and sister immediately picked her up and escorted her out of the church. As everyone was leaving to go to the burial, I felt this weird breeze go through my body. It was like Wil was telling me to snap out of it and be strong. I got into the family car, and we headed to the burial. Once we arrived, everyone stepped back so that we could stand close to the casket. The pastor spoke about Wil and asked everyone to pray for the family. Everyone was given a flower to place on his casket. Kendal stayed in the car at the burial site. She stared out the window until it was all over.

I thought I wasn't going to be able to handle it, but we celebrated his life, and I truly believed Wil was comforting me from Heaven. Out of nowhere, I felt this sense of relief, which made everything easier to deal with.

"Rest in peace, Wil. I love you," I whispered.

After the funeral, I found out that my brother, Wil, had actually been murdered by his girlfriend, Kendal's, supposed ex-boyfriend. His name was Mack Sims, and he was a straight thug. He had a criminal record a mile long, and he wasn't even a student at the college. Apparently, they had been at a party off campus, some words had been exchanged between Wil and this Mack character, and a fight had broken out. During the fight, someone had started shooting, and Wil had been struck in his stomach. By the time the ambulance arrived, he had lost too much blood. They tried to save him, but he died an hour after he arrived at the hospital.

Kendal had been nowhere to be found at the crime scene, but she had apparently been at the party that night. She didn't even have the decency to act like she cared for my brother. I hated her for that. Mack was named as a suspect and picked up by the local police. I wasn't allowed to go to the trial, but it took its toll on my parents. Although they had a lot of support from family and friends, they were emotionally, financially, and mentally drained. Everything was changing. Mack claimed self-defense, and because no one would come forward as a witness to testify against him, he got off. He also claimed the gun used in the shooting was not his. Mack said that Wil had started the fight because he was upset that he and Kendal had broken up, and she'd gone back to him. He said Wil had kept punching him, and he'd feared for his life. He'd seen the gun just lying on the ground and had taken his chances. Vanessa told my family and the detective that she and Wil were getting back together and that Kendal had become obsessed and had started threatening Wil. She said Kendal had even called her and told her to stay the hell away from Wil, or there was going to be trouble. Supposedly, Kendal had lied to her ex-boyfriend Mack and had said that Wil had hit her, so Mack had gone to the party to seek revenge. Unfortunately, it wasn't enough to substantiate the evidence against Mack, because it was circumstantial.

During the trial, Kendal was again missing in action and refused to defend my brother's position, which led me to believe Vanessa's side

Chapter 6

Disappearing Acts

Jaylen

I was awakened by a knock on the door. The room service I'd ordered last night had arrived as scheduled. I greeted the waiter at the door because I wanted to surprise Toni before she woke up. I handed him a tip and proceeded to set up the breakfast platters on my own. I lifted the lids to make sure everything that I had ordered was accounted for. The coffee was piping hot, and the fruit appeared to be fresh. I decided that I would wake Toni up so she could enjoy her surprise.

"Wake up, Mrs. Payne." She didn't move, so I shook her. "Toni, breakfast is waiting, so please get up."

She finally rolled over, rubbed her eyes, and lifted herself up onto the pillows. "Wow, Jaylen.

This is just so nice of you. You didn't have to do this, but thank you."

"Well, I know we kinda got off to a rocky start yesterday, so I wanted to start off on a good note this morning."

"Well, let me brush my teeth before I eat. My mouth tastes stale."

It seemed as though she was in a good mood. I walked up behind her in the bathroom and hugged her and kissed her gently on the neck. She seemed to like it, so I proceeded to kiss her all over. Before I knew it, we were making love in the bathroom. We eventually made our way out to the bed and then onto the floor. We went at it. She was so passionate and intense. I didn't ever remember seeing this side of her. After about thirty minutes of going at it, we exchanged multiple orgasms. I wore her out and she wore me out. We lay there for a few more minutes, but then we decided to get up and eat because we knew that our breakfast was getting cold.

We both sat at the table and devoured our food. The food was slammin'. After we ate, we lay down again on the bed.

"So what got into you?" I asked.

"You got into me, Mr. Payne."

"Well, you know what they say. No pain, no gain."

"Yeah, whatever," she replied and laughed.

"So, what do you want to do today? Your wish is my command, baby."

"I'm ready for round two. So what do you want to do?"

"Girl, you ain't said nothing."

This time around I took more control over the situation. After about fifteen minutes, she was begging me to stop. I had to put my thing down. We must have changed positions at least a dozen times.

"Jay, please stop. I'm tired and you're hurting me," she said.

"Are you serious? I'm just getting started."

She gave me a look that said, "You've got to be kidding me." It was obvious that I could have kept going and going and going, but because she was my wife, I would respect her wishes.

"Is everything okay?" I asked.

"Yeah, I guess I overdid it the first round, so I couldn't keep up this time."

"I understand. You'll have plenty of time to make it up to me."

"I know and I will."

"Do you want to lie out on the deck after you get yourself together?" I asked.

"Not right now, but you can go and get some sun. You wore me out, so I need to take a nap, if you don't mind."

"Well, I don't mind staying here with you."

"No, baby. Go have some fun in the sun. I'll join you later."

"I forgot to tell you that I hit the jackpot on the dollar slot machines last night."

"For how much?" she asked.

"Five hundred dollars."

"Five hundred dollars?"

"On top of that, I had just won three hundred and fifty dollars at the craps table," I bragged.

"Can I go shopping?"

"Sure. When do you want to go?"

"Later on, after my nap."

"It sounds good to me. Just get plenty of rest, because I'm feeling lucky again, and I want to go back to the casino."

"All right Jaylen. Make sure you lock the cabin, and please put the DO NOT DISTURB sign outside, on the door, so that the maids do not come in here and bother me," she ordered.

I grabbed my towel, iPod, and sunblock and headed for the deck. I needed to soak up some sun and relaxation. The ship was in the middle of nowhere, and it felt like a floating city with malls, casinos, and restaurants. There was a main attraction every night. I didn't think seven days was enough time for us to do everything I wanted to do. I sure hoped Toni liked getting on water rides, because I was a big kid at heart, and it looked like a lot of fun.

As I lay there listening to my iPod, there were so many songs that reminded me of Joi. I just couldn't stop thinking about her, but I knew I had to. I needed to continue moving on. Toni and I had some kinks we needed to work out, but I was willing to try.

As usual, I dozed off for what seemed like forever, but it was hardly an hour later when I woke up. I figured that I would go and convince Toni to come and lie out on the deck with me. This way she could relax and nap, and we could spend some quality time together. As I got up to go back to our cabin, I saw a woman who resembled Toni, but on the other side of the deck. I could not tell if it was Toni, because of the way she was standing. I just brushed it off because Toni had been exhausted not even an hour ago and this person was all up in some man's face.

When I approached the cabin, I noticed the DO NOT DISTURB sign still on the door. I opened the door with my key, and Toni was nowhere to be found. I thoroughly checked our cabin, and she was gone. All of a sudden, I remembered that the woman on the deck who had had her back turned toward me had looked a lot like Toni. Yet, I was confused, because if that was her, then who was the man?

"I need some answers," I said aloud.

I quickly changed into some shorts and a Dallas Cowboys T-shirt. I went back to the area where I had seen the woman who looked like Toni from the back, but she was gone. I decided to look in areas away from the deck to see if I bumped into her. As usual, my wife was nowhere to be found, and I could not find the woman or man I'd seen earlier. I started having some messed-up thoughts in my head.

Is Toni cheating on me with someone on the ship? I mean, she made the reservations, I angrily thought to myself. *Maybe the reason why I can never find her is that she is in another man's cabin.*

I decided to do a little detective work on my own. I went back to the cabin, and she was still not there, so I put the DO NOT DISTURB sign back up. I positioned myself in a corner of the suite so that she could not see me when she came in. About fifteen minutes later, I heard the door unlock. I heard Toni making some noise, as if she was getting undressed. I stepped out from the corner a few minutes later, and she had managed to jump back in the bed and under the covers. She wanted me to think that she had been there all the time.

"Toni!" I yelled.

She jumped up when I called her name, and she even had the nerve to try to look sleepy. "What the hell is wrong with you, and why are you yelling?"

"No, the question should be, where in the hell were you?"

"Here in bed, trying to take a damn nap, Jaylen," she said flatly.

"So, you're going to sit here and tell me that you've been here all the time?"

"That's exactly what I'm telling you."

"Toni, I'm going to ask you one more time. Where were you?"

"Here," she repeated.

"So I must look like Boo Boo the fool."

"What is your problem?"

"Toni, you were not in this room when I got here," I said testily.

"Oh, that's what you're talking about. I had just stepped out for about two minutes to see if there was a vending machine near the cabin."

"Just two minutes?"

"Yeah, Jay. You must have just missed me, but I came right back."

"Toni, you're lying. You were gone for over thirty minutes, and I could have sworn I saw you all up in some brotha's face out on the deck."

"Now you are hallucinating."

"No, Toni, you are. I can't believe you're trying to play me like this," I huffed.

"Play you? Negro, you've been playing me. All I am to you is a replacement for Miss Perfect Little Joi. I'm the one who should be insulted. I can't compete against her, and I will not play second fiddle to some man-stealing ho."

"Oh, so now this is about my relationship with Joi. You're the one with the ex-husband. I am not going to sit here and pretend that I don't care about her, and I am not going to sit here and play games with you. I'm sure you still care for Kenyatta, or whatever the hell his name is. We both rushed into this marriage knowing we had baggage, but I was willing to work at it. All I need to know is whether or not you are having an affair."

"No, Jaylen, I am not having an affair," Toni insisted. "So, where do we go from here?"

"I'm not sure. I refuse to be the only one trying to make things work between us," I said.

"I would like to try, too. I won't mention Joi's name again."

I sat down on the couch to collect my thoughts. I turned on the television to take my mind off of what had just happened. I didn't know what to think. I told Toni that I was going over to the casino and that she was more than welcome to come with me. This time she didn't refuse.

Toni was quiet the entire walk over, and I really wasn't saying much, either. The casino was crowded again. I went over to the dollar slots, and I had to wait around to play my same machine. There was an elderly woman playing the machine, and she refused to get up. She just kept loading up the machine with one-hundred-dollar bills. I felt bad for her because she was trying to hit the jackpot and the machine kept taking her money.

"This damn machine ain't doing nothing. I've been playing for over an hour, and I've lost close to four hundred dollars. I hate to leave all my money in this machine, but you just gotta know when to quit," she said.

She grabbed her purse and got up from the machine. I couldn't wait. Toni was playing the quarter slots over on the other side. I put one hundred dollars into the machine, and after only two pulls, I hit for twelve hundred dollars. I couldn't believe it. The bells were going off, and people started standing around my machine.

The same little old lady came back over to the machine. She couldn't believe it.

"Congratulations," she said.

"Thank you," I replied.

"Just my luck. I walk away and you hit," she added, with a sigh. "Well, at least somebody hit that old machine. Oh boy, I just can't believe it. I'm so mad, I could cry."

The machine attendant came and counted out twelve crisp one-hundred-dollar bills. I felt bad for the elderly lady. I had seen her put at least four hundred dollars in this machine. She went and sat down and started digging for some change to play the nickel slots. I walked away, and she smiled at me. I went to tell Toni about my jackpot win, but she had left the quarter slots to go over to the blackjack table. I walked around for about fifteen to twenty minutes, and I bumped back into the woman who had lost her money. She looked desperate and was playing the penny slots by now. I knew there was a reason I'd won this money, so there had to be a reason why I did what I did next. I walked over to the elderly woman and tapped her on her shoulder.

"Excuse me, ma'am. I'm the man who played your machine after you left."

"Yes, what can I do for you?" she said.

"Here's the four hundred dollars you lost in that machine."

"Are you serious?" she gasped.

"Absolutely. I watched you put your money in that machine, so it's only fair that I return your money. I won twelve hundred dollars, and that was more than enough for me."

"God bless you. Oh my gosh! Oh my gosh! I didn't know what I was going to do. My husband would have killed me if he knew I had lost all of our vacation money."

"Well, now that you have it back, just try not to lose it all again. I'm just saying," I advised.

"No way. I'm going back to my cabin right now. Can I just give you a big ole hug?"

By the time this lady stopped hugging me, she was in tears. I watched her scurry her way out of the casino. I was just happy that I could give her back her money. I went to search for my wife, and she was still at the blackjack table. She appeared to be having a good time, and based on the stack of chips in front of her, it was obvious that she was winning. An hour later, the night was winding down, and we left the casino. Toni wanted to go and listen to the jazz band in the lobby. We stayed there for a little while, then ate a light dinner and went back to the cabin.

As we made our way back to our cabin, we saw people getting off the ship. We were finally in the Bahamas. We could come and go as we pleased for three days. The ship was docked in the heart of Nassau, behind the Best Western Hotel. I personally couldn't wait to get off the ship. I was starting to feel seasick. Toni and I just got off the ship with everybody else. We discovered a McDonald's and a KFC five minutes away from where we were docked. The cars were driven on the opposite side of the street, which was confusing as hell. There were straw markets everywhere you turned, and they knew how to work the tourists.

"Hello, beau-ti-ful la-dy. Would you like to buy something? We sell T-shirts, hats, dresses," a woman said, with a Bahamian accent.

"How much?" Toni asked.

"Two for fifteen dollars," the woman informed her.

"No, thank you. I'm just looking," said Toni.

"Is that your husband?"

"Yes."

"He is a handsome fella. You two make a beau-ti-ful couple."

"Boy, she knows how to pour the compliments on thick. I know I look good. So I don't need anybody trying to tell me something I already know so I can buy a damn T-shirt," Toni whispered to me.

"Toni, just buy something. These women and men work hard. They have to hand make most of their items just to make a living," I told her.

"Well, you buy something."

"Excuse me. I would like to buy two T-shirts for fifteen dollars," I told the woman. "I need an extra large for me and a large for my wife."

"I don't wear a large. I wear a medium," Toni said.

"Sorry. Can you exchange the large for a medium please?" I asked the woman.

She handed me the shirts as I gave her a twenty-dollar bill.

"Thank you, and keep the change," I said.

"Oh. Thank you, sir."

We continued to make our way downtown. The white people were getting their hair braided and paying big money for it. Toni asked one white lady how much it had cost to get three cornrows on the side of her head, and the lady said, "Thirty dollars."

"Thirty dollars?" Toni repeated.

"Yes, it's ten dollars a cornrow," the lady replied.

"If you don't mind me asking, where are you from?" said Toni.

"I'm from New York," the lady told her.

"You can get probably get your whole head done for thirty dollars in New York," Toni said.

"I know, but we just get it done for fun when we come here on vacation. I don't wear the braids when I'm home."

This was why the Africans over in the States need to come to the Bahamas and start doing hair. They'd save half the time and do three times the number of heads. Toni and I continued walking downtown. We stopped off at a liquor store to purchase some Bahamian wine to take back home. The prices were reasonable, so I purchased four bottles of their finest wines.

Finally, we arrived in the more elite part of town. They had Coach stores as well as other top designers. Toni was like a kid in a candy store.

"Jay, look at these sandals. They are to die for."

"How much are they?" I asked.

"One hundred twenty-five dollars."

"Tell the saleslady your size. It's my treat."

"Excuse me. Do you have these in a size eight and a half?" Toni asked the saleslady.

"Yes, we do," the saleslady replied.

"Thanks, baby," Toni said, when kissing me on the cheek.

I paid for her sandals, and we continued walking around. I stopped at a nearby jewelry store and treated myself to an inexpensive watch. We had thought about taking a cab from Nassau over to Paradise Island, but we decided to wait until tomorrow. It was getting late, so we headed back to the ship. I wanted to try the conch salad because I had heard that it was good. That would just have to wait until tomorrow, too.

The next morning we got up, and for the first time, we ate breakfast in the restaurant on the ship. They had everything you could think of. There were homemade waffles with banana syrup and/or strawberry syrup. They would make you special-order omelets. I just piled a little bit of everything on my plate. We didn't have to pay, either. Well, not exactly, because it was included in the price of the trip. After breakfast, we went for a power walk along the beach. The water was aqua blue. It looked like Kool-aid. People were riding on this thing called a banana boat. It was an inflated, banana-shaped boat that was hooked onto a regular boat and dragged all around in the water. It looked like fun, but I passed.

We spent the rest of the day riding mopeds and touring Nassau. The state buildings and hospitals were painted in bright green colors. There was even an Elks Lodge. We met a man named Winston Churchill, and he knew some of my relatives in the States. He went out of his way to accommodate us. He invited us to church. He also took us to this restaurant called Tony Roma's. They served barbecued ribs and barbecued chicken, which was right up our alley. Their food was slammin'. I ate everything on my plate.

Our last night in the Bahamas was fun. We finally made our way to Paradise Island. We had to cross this weird-shaped bridge to get there. Once we were on Paradise Island, I couldn't wait to try my luck at the casino, but Toni wanted to go dancing. Lucky for us, the club was in the casino. She stayed next to me for a good five minutes, until she heard the music from the club.

"Jaylen, I'll be back. They're in there jamming. Don't leave me hanging."

"I won't," I assured her.

I played the slots, and I wasn't hitting anything. I was down six hundred dollars. I went over to the craps table and the table was so cold and everyone, including me, crapped out.

"What in the hell just happened? I just lost one thousand dollars," I said aloud.

I didn't even know how to break the news to my wife. All I had left was about fifty dollars to my name. What in the hell was I going to do? I knew I had promised Toni that I would come in and dance with her, but I was not in the mood to party. I went and found myself a chair and sat down. I was devastated. Almost two hours had gone by, and I didn't have the energy to find my wife, but I needed to. As I got up and started walking toward the club, I bumped into the same elderly woman who had lost her money on the ship. This time she was all dressed up. Her hair was done. She looked completely different. The older gentleman on her arm must have been her husband, because he was decked out too.

"Well, hello Mister?" said the woman. "I'm sorry. I didn't catch your name the other evening."

"Jaylen Payne, and yours?" I replied.

"Daisy Lynn Felton, and this is my husband, Bill."

"Hello. Nice to meet you. So, you look great," I said. "How is everything going?"

"I feel fabulous! What about you?" said Daisy.

"As well as expected."

"How come you're not playing the slots?" asked Daisy.

"Oh, I'm just waiting for my wife," I lied.

"Yeah, I bet you are. You must have lost your money," Daisy concluded. "Believe me, I know how you feel. You look like I looked the other night. You can't fool me. Now, what did you say your name was again? Jayden? How much did you lose?"

"No, that's Jaylen, j-a-y-l-e-n. And I lost one thousand dollars."

"Oh, I'm sorry, Jaylen. Is your last name spelled like the word *pain,* as in *pain reliever*?"

"Actually, that is not how my last name is spelled," I said.

"Well, how else would anybody spell *pain*?" asked Daisy.

"P-a-y-n-e."

"Oh, please accept my apology. I'm a little older than you. Just a little." She laughed.

I couldn't help but laugh. She had actually lifted my spirits. I had finally stopped feeling sorry for myself. We said our good-byes, and I went to the club and danced with my wife. I was glad because we both needed to burn some energy. As we made our way out of the casino, I bumped back into Mrs. Daisy Lynn Felton again.

"Wow. Is this old lady following me?" I muttered to myself.

"Is this your wife, Jaylen?" Daisy said, smiling.

"Yes, she is, Miss Daisy Lynn Felton," I replied.

"Hi. I'm Toni."

"Miss Toni, you've got a good man there," Daisy remarked. "He really took good care of me, and I was a complete stranger."

"Oh, really? He did?" Toni said, looking confused.

"Well, Jaylen, I never forget acts of kindness from people like yourself," Daisy declared. "So here is a little something for you because if you had not done for me whatcha did, I would not be where I am at today. Here's a token of my appreciation, Mr. Jaylen Payne. J-a-y-l-e-n P-a-y-n-e." She winked.

As she walked away, I opened the envelope, and inside there was a check for four hundred thousand dollars payable to Jaylen Payne. There was a note inside that said: *Because of your act of kindness, I took one hundred dollars out of the money you gave me, and I hit the jackpot for two and a half million dollars. I owe you so much. So please accept this gesture on my behalf, and God bless you. You lost a thousand dollars tonight, and because you gave me four hundred dollars, I took your loss and multiplied it by the amount you gave to me. Thank you so much. I postdated the check by fourteen days because I need to handle the deposit on my end with Wachovia Bank when we get back. After that, the money is all yours. Enjoy, Daisy.*

I couldn't believe it. Toni just went into a state of shock.

"Jaylen, what just happened back there? Did that old lady just give you a check for four hundred thousand dollars?"

"Yes, she did."

"Four hundred thousand dollars?" Toni repeated.

"That's what it says. Somebody pinch me, because I must be dreaming."

"I don't believe it. This is just too crazy. Oh my gosh, is that check real?"

"I believe so. I guess we'll find out when I go cash it. I just have to wait for two weeks, when the funds become available."

"You're going to have to pay a lot of taxes on that money, Jaylen."

"Yeah, that's a bummer, but I'll still net a decent amount," I noted.

"I mean, tell me what happened, Jaylen."

"It's a long story that I'll be happy to share with you on our way back home."

"Now we can buy a big house and a brand-new Mercedes Benz for me."

"Calm down, Toni. I don't even have the money yet, and if I did, my intention is not to blow it. I would like to put some of it into my investment firm and save some for retirement."

"What about a house?" she asked.

"Toni, we can use some of the money to put a down payment on a house. However, we need to stay in an affordable price range."

"Well, aren't I entitled to half or something?" Toni asked.

"I already told you what I'm doing with the money, and why would you be entitled to half?"

At this point, all Toni wanted to discuss was the money I got. I was still in a state of shock, and I needed a moment to digest it all. Toni and I headed back to the ship. She wanted me to hold her hand as we made our way to our cabin.

"Jaylen, can we just go for a quiet, romantic

walk around the ship tonight? We haven't had a chance to hold hands and sightsee since we've been here. I mean, I know our honeymoon started out a little rocky, but I want us to get a fresh start, because I really love you."

"I guess we can," I replied.

"When we get back, I would like to give you a full body massage and finish where we left off the other day. Okay?"

"Wow. What did I do so special to deserve all of this?"

"You don't have to do anything, baby. I'm your wife, and it is my job to take care of my man."

"Well, it's my job to make sure I take care of you, too."

"You got that right," she said.

Our ship was set to sail at 7:00 sharp the next morning, and it was leaving with or without passengers. The captain made it crystal clear that everyone needed to be back on the ship an hour before it was scheduled to leave. They were going to give two warnings, which they demonstrated before people got off the ship. With that said, there would be no excuses unless it was a life-or-death situation. Overall, this evening had turned out to be the best so far, and I didn't have any plans of giving this money back to the casino.

Toni and I went for a romantic walk out on the deck. We stopped and took pictures and listened to the jazz band play a few songs. It was dark outside, but you could still see parts of Nassau. I could hear people laughing and having a good time on the dinner cruises, which seemed to run every hour on the hour. You could hear the Bahamian music from a distance. There was so much to do on these islands and so little time. I was just going to visit the Bahamas next year. I wanted to stay at the Atlantis, a resort on Paradise Island, because it had a lot to offer, and I wanted to make up for lost time.

There were several couples out on the deck. They were holding hands, kissing, and dancing. Others were scattered throughout the ship. Toni pressed her body up against mine, and we started kissing. Out of nowhere, she became this loving and caring person. I just went along with it, because I was still trying to figure out her motives. As I looked around, I noticed an African American man just staring down at us. He was a dark-complexioned brotha, and he looked to be around six feet tall or so. I could not tell if he had dreads or braids in his hair, but they were long. He stood there for a few more seconds, and then he walked away. I didn't think any more of it.

We finally made our way back to the cabin. Once we got inside, Toni poured us some wine and ordered room service. She put a Gerald Levert and Teena Marie CD in the player and lit candles everywhere.

"Jaylen, let me undress you so that I can give you a full body massage," Toni offered. "The food won't be here for at least an hour, so we have time."

"I can take off my own clothes, Toni."

"I know, but I want to take them off here and right now."

She took off my shirt and then my shorts and boxers. I stood there, looking down at her, with my sneakers still on my feet. She looked back up at me.

"Lie down, baby. I'll take off your sneakers," she whispered.

She took off my sneakers, and then she asked me to lie down on my stomach. As I turned over, she was putting some massage oil in her hands. She started massaging my neck and back. I ain't gonna lie. This shit was feeling good. Toni worked me over. She didn't miss a beat. I had almost fallen asleep when someone knocked on the door.

"Who is it?" Toni asked.

"It's room service," said a female voice.

"I'll be right there," Toni called.

Toni rolled the food in by herself. I heard the woman say thank you, which indicated to me that she had received a tip. I guess Toni didn't want her to come in since I was not dressed. She had ordered filet mignon, lobster tails, garlic mashed potatoes and broccoli. We ate like there was no tomorrow. The food was absolutely delicious. Toni and I each drank two glasses of white wine. It just topped off the entire meal.

Wow. A romantic walk, a full body massage, followed by a delicious meal. What more coud I ask for? I thought to myself.

"Come on, Jaylen. I said I wanted us to finish where we left off the other day," said Toni.

I turned around, and Toni was completely nude. All she had on was a pair of red stilettos, and "Fire and Desire" by Teena Marie and Rick James was playing on the CD player. She started slow dancing by herself while making seductive gestures with her body toward me, and I went along with it for a few minutes. Then she started kissing me all over and doing things I couldn't even repeat. Toni had skills, but I needed to show her what I was bringing to the table again. I picked her up and propped her legs around my waist and wore her out for about twenty minutes. She tried to hang in there and go toe-to-toe, but it was obvious that it was too much. I slowed down and laid her across the bed, where I continued to make love to her.

"Okay, Jaylen. That's enough. You're hurting my stomach," she said.

"Come on, baby. I'm almost there. I just need a few more seconds."

"Oh please, Jaylen. We can finish later."

"Wait, Toni. I'm comin' now, baby. Ahh."

Afterwards, I just lay there thinking about everything. Toni had never complained this much before we got married. Maybe she needed to go and see a doctor or something to make sure she was all right. I held her in my arms until we both fell asleep.

I got up around 6:30 a.m. and walked out on the deck. I wanted to get another look at the island before we left. The ship had already given the first warning signal. I noticed only one couple getting on board. I knew Toni had no intention of getting up for at least another couple of hours, so I decided to read the magazines near the swimming pools. From a distance, I could see somebody walking in my direction. As they got closer, I saw that it was the brotha who had been looking down in my direction yesterday.

"What's up?" the brotha said while extending his hand to shake mine.

"What's up?" I said while shaking his hand.

"I guess we're the only two brothas up this early."

"Yeah, it looks that way."

"I'm sorry, man. My name is K. J. And yours?"

"It's Jaylen," I said.

"Well, nice to meet you. Is this your first time on a cruise?" K. J. quizzed.

"Well, yeah. Is it yours?"

"Nah, I take one at least once a year."

"Well, it's my honeymoon, and my wife wanted to go on a cruise," I replied.

"Congratulations, man. My wife and I came together, but just for a vacation."

"How long you been married?"

"Almost five years," said K. J.

"Yeah, I saw you yesterday on the top deck, but I don't think I saw your wife. I only recognized you because there's only a handful of brothas on this ship."

"Nah, my wife was sleeping, and if she ain't sleeping, she's shopping. What about yours?"

"Same deal. She's either shopping or shopping some more, then sleeping."

"Hey, maybe we can all meet up one night for dinner before we dock in Miami," K. J. suggested.

"That's cool with me."

"All right. Peace man."

"We'll catch up with you later."

He seemed to be cool. Shit, his wife and my wife would have made a great team, considering that they liked the same things. Oh, well, the cruise was almost over now.

I stayed out on the deck a little while longer and then went back to the cabin. When I walked in, Toni was leaned over the toilet, vomiting.

"Toni, are you all right?" I asked.

"Yeah, I just have an upset stomach," she moaned.

"Well, you don't feel warm, but you do look flushed. Do you think it might be food poisoning?"

"No, silly. We ate the same thing, and you're fine."

"Well, what could it be?"

"I think I might be pregnant," she murmured.

"Pregnant?"

"Yes, Jaylen, pregnant. I missed my period, but I thought it was because of my nerves surrounding the wedding."

"Wow. I'm sorry. I'm just a little shocked by the news," I confessed.

"I don't know why you would be shocked. You are always pressuring me about having a baby."

"Is something wrong with wanting to have a son or daughter?" I asked.

"No, but I do have a very demanding job, Jaylen."

"We have plenty of time to figure it all out."

"Wow, that money you just got will come in handy, and it was right on time, because a baby is expensive."

"Well, before we get ahead of ourselves, you need to make sure. I will go and purchase a pregnancy test, and you just try to get some rest. I'll be right back."

I left and went to the main deck to see where I could purchase a pregnancy test. I didn't know what to think. It was not like we weren't having intercourse before we got married, so it made sense that she could be pregnant.

I was looking around, and I bumped right into K. J. He was by himself, so I guessed his wife was still asleep.

"What's up? Jaylen, right?"

"Yeah, man."

"Did you get a chance to talk to your wife about all of us meeting up for dinner?" he asked.

"No, not yet, but I'm sure we can make something happen," I said.

"You all right, man?"

"Yeah, I'm just looking for someplace on this boat where you can buy aspirin and stuff."

"Your wife sick?" K. J. asked.

"No, she might be pregnant, and I need to buy a pregnancy test."

"Wow, uh . . . congratulations. Didn't you just get married?"

"Man, you know how it is. It's not like we became celibate a month or two before the wedding. It probably was the same for you and your wife."

"Yeah, you're right. We might be expecting a child, too," he confessed.

"For real? What a coincidence," I said.

"Well, uh, I gotta go. Peace."

After K. J. left, I walked around until I came across a store that sold a little bit of everything. The store had one pregnancy test, which cost $12.99. I paid for the test and went back to the cabin. I gave Toni the pregnancy test, and she took it with her into the bathroom. I never got a chance to tell her about K. J. and his wife wanting to have dinner with us. After about ten minutes, Toni came out of the bathroom.

"So, what did the test show?" I asked.

"I'm pregnant."

"Yes!" I shouted.

Toni looked more annoyed than happy. I wanted to ask her what was wrong, but I could tell that she really didn't want to talk about it. Maybe that was the reason she was hurting during intercourse. I didn't know, but as soon as we got back, she was going to the doctor.

Chapter 7

Right Gone Wrong?

Faith

It had been a couple of days since I last talked to Tyree. He said he had been busy running around with his mother. I'd been busy studying for my nursing school exams. I didn't know how I had managed to hang in there this long, but I couldn't wait until it was over. I was going to celebrate for an entire month. I hadn't talked to my girl Joi in a minute. I knew she'd been going through some stuff. I just hoped Jaylen's wedding hadn't taken a toll on her. It was just a shame that their relationship had ended. They'd been the ideal couple in college. It was like they were made for each other. They'd been the couple everybody wanted to be like.

Ring.

"Hello? Hello? Who's calling?" I asked.

"Girl, what you mean, who's calling? It's your boy Tyree."

"Oh, well, next time say something."

"I did. You just didn't hear me," he said.

"So what's up, Tyree? I haven't heard from you in a couple of days."

"Well, I told you that I had some things that I had to do for my mother."

"I know. I was just saying."

"Are you busy tonight?" he asked.

"No. Why?"

"I figured we could go see that new movie with Will Smith."

"That's cool with me. I need a break from all of this studying. So, Tyree, do you want me to come to your house, and we can leave from there?"

"Not today. Next time you can come over here to my crib. I'm already in your area, so I'll save you the trip."

"You always say that. Why is it that you can come over here, but I can't come to your house?" I asked.

"It's not like that, Faith. I'm just not home right now. Don't take it personal. You'll get to come to my house."

"What time is the movie?"

"I think it starts at four thirty."

"Well, we have almost two hours before it starts," I said.

"Well, then that will be one more hour in which we get to know each other better."

"Are you hungry?" I asked.

"Yeah, I'm hungry. Are you going to cook me something to eat?"

"I'll make you some turkey burgers. That's all I have in my refrigerator. I need to go shopping."

"All right. I'll see you in a few."

Something was definitely going on with Tyree. He always wanted to come to my house, but the mere mention that I wanted to go over to his house made him start trippin'. Maybe he had a girlfriend or something and didn't want me to know, because he was no damn good, or maybe his house was dirty and he was ashamed. Whatever the problem was, I was going to get to the bottom of it. I was going to tell him that he needed to buy me some groceries. I didn't mind cooking for him, but my budget was tight since I was still in school.

Ding-dong.

"Coming!" I yelled.

I peeked through the peephole, and it was Tyree. I opened the door, and he grabbed me and just started kissing me for no reason.

"What has gotten into you?" I scolded.

"It's you, Faith. I just miss my baby."

"If you say so, Tyree."

"Girl, come here. What's wrong?"

"You know what's wrong with me," I said.

"No, I do not."

"Tyree, what are you hiding from me? You never want me over at your house, and you're always coming over here. I mean, I don't mind, but sometimes I need a change of atmosphere. I know you're not ashamed of me, because I look too damn good for that. So what is it?"

"I guess I'm just ashamed of my house," he admitted.

"Come on, Tyree. You know I'm not like that."

"I know. I promise we can go over to my crib next week."

"Okay, Tyree. I'm going to hold you to that. Your burgers will be ready in a minute. Do you want something to drink?"

"Yeah. What do you have?"

"I have water and lemonade," I told him.

"I'll take the lemonade."

I gave Tyree his two turkey burgers along with some lemonade. He must have finished his food in less than three minutes. If he thought he was going to sit here and eat me out of house and home, he was crazy.

Burp. "Excuse me," said Tyree.

"You're excused."

"Faith, are you ready to go now?"

"Yes. I just hate missing the first part of the movie."

I got into Tyree's truck, and we headed to the movie theater. The line was long, so he dropped me off to get the tickets.

"Faith, run and get in line while I park," he said as I jumped out.

"Okay, but I need some money first."

I paid for the tickets and waited for Tyree to come so that we could go inside. I peeked

through the window at the parking lot and no
Tyree. Finally, he walked up behind me, with this
crazy look in his eyes.

"Were you looking for me?" he asked.

"Yes, I was. You had me waiting around and
looking for yo' ass."

Tyree started laughing, and there wasn't shit
funny. I liked him a lot, but he was so inconsiderate and immature. We chose seats toward the
back of the movie theater. People were still walking in with popcorn and soda. I didn't recall
seeing the previews of the movie, but if Will
Smith was in it, it should be good. The movie
lasted for about an hour and a half. It was a good
movie, as I'd suspected. It was an action-packed
thriller. We made our way out of the movie theater. Tyree asked me if I wanted to go and get
something to eat, since I hadn't eaten yet.

"Sure," I said.

"What are you in the mood for?"

"Can we go to T.G.I. Friday's?"

"It doesn't matter to me."

On our way to the restaurant, we passed a lot
of other places that we could have stopped at.
I thought of suggesting another place so that
he wouldn't have to drive around, but I didn't
say anything. As Tyree was driving, it seemed
as if someone recognized him, because a car
beeped at us. Tyree just took off. I knew where
T.G.I. Friday's was located, but he took us out
of the way.

"Who was that?" I asked.

"Who was who?"

"Somebody was blowing their horn at you, and you took off in another direction, Tyree. I am not stupid," I snapped.

"Look, Faith, I don't need to listen to this shit."

"Well, just take me home. I'm not hungry."

"All right. I'm not going to kiss your ass, Faith," he snarled.

He turned the truck around and sped to my house. When his truck pulled up, I jumped out. I had had it with Tyree. There were just way too many questions in my head, and I liked him too much to get hurt.

"Faith?"

"What, Tyree?"

"Can I talk to you?"

"About what, Tyree? Look, you need to leave. You know how much I like you, and you're playing with my feelings. All this shit doesn't add up, and you keep lying to me."

"Yo, Faith. I'm sorry. I do care about you and don't want to hurt you. I want to get to know you better. Please, let's start over."

Tyree sounded so sincere, and I wanted to believe him. He came into my house, and we just chilled out by watching some movies on the DVD player. I sat really close to him, and every now and then, he would lean over and kiss me. I got up and walked into the kitchen, and he followed me. We started kissing again, and this time he took off his shirt. There were too many muscles for me to count. I knew that if he did not put that shirt back on, I might end up doing something that I would regret.

"Tyree, please put your shirt back on."

"I'd rather keep it off. It's starting to get hot up in here."

The next thing I knew, he had me pinned up against the refrigerator, and I couldn't move. I was just about to take my blouse off when I came to my senses.

"Stop it. Please get off me," I told him.

"Why'd you push me away?"

"Because this is not the way I want you, Tyree. I am so attracted to you that it scares me, but I am vulnerable right now, which makes me an easy target."

"I'm not going to hurt you. I care about you too much."

"Well, if you care about me so much, let's take it slow," I said.

"If that's the way you want it."

"Yeah, that's the way it has to be."

Whew. I had come so close to giving all of myself away to this man. It had taken every ounce of strength I had in me not to give in. I mean every ounce of me.

"Well, I'm going to let myself out," Tyree announced.

"Okay."

"I will call you later."

As I watched him walk out that door, I felt like that might be the last time I saw him.

* * *

He didn't call me, like he'd said he would. I didn't hear from Tyree for a whole week. I left numerous messages on his phone, and he never returned my calls. I was hurt because he had only confirmed my suspicions that he wanted only one thing. I was just glad I hadn't given in.

I got up this morning, and I was feeling a little depressed. I figured that I would call Joi, because she would know what to say to make me feel better. I knew that I could have called Taj or Eboni, but they didn't know me like Joi knew me.

Ring.

"Hello?"

"Joi?"

"Hey, Faith. What's up? I haven't heard from you in a minute. I figured you were busy with your new beau. So how's everything going?"

"It's not going. I think he's mad at me. I haven't heard from him in over a week."

I filled Joi in on all the details, and she just listened at first. She didn't try to judge me. Based on what I told her, she felt that Tyree had something to hide. She knew I had developed some strong feelings for him, because I started crying on the telephone.

"Faith, are you in love with this man?"

"I think I am, Joi."

"Oh Lord."

"Why did you say that?" I asked.

"Because I don't want to see you get hurt."

"Joi, I know that he likes me a lot, but maybe he is trapped in another situation."

"Well, he needs to be up front and honest with you about it. He should not lead you on."

"I agree."

"Do you want me to call him?" she asked.

"No. If he doesn't want to call me back, that is his choice," I replied.

"Okay, if you say so. Are you going to be all right? Do you need me to come over there?"

"No, I'll be fine, but thanks."

I hung up the telephone, and I started to feel a little better. I went into the kitchen to fix myself something to eat, and then the doorbell rang. As I peeked through the peephole, I recognized the person on the other side of the door. It was Tyree. As I opened the door, I could tell something was wrong.

"Hey, Tyree. Is everything okay? I've been worried about you."

"I'm sorry, baby. I should have called," he said.

"It's okay. You're here now."

"I never want to lose you. You're the best thing that has ever happened to me. When you turned me away, I let my pride get the best of me. I do have a lot of things going on right now in my life, but I don't want to get into that. I came here today to apologize to you for acting like a little boy last week."

"I accept your apology, Tyree. I just want you to know that I'm here for you, but just be straight with me. Okay?"

"Okay. So did you eat yet?"

"No, I was just about to fix myself something to eat when the doorbell rang."

"Can I take you to T.G.I. Friday's to make up for the last time?"

"I'd like that, Tyree."

"And I like you."

This time we drove directly to the restaurant. Tyree came around and opened the car door for me like a perfect gentleman. We went inside and ordered from the appetizer menu. I ordered some buffalo wings and fries, and he ordered a turkey burger. We ate our food and drank a couple of sodas. I had so much fun. We stopped by the park on our way back and talked some more. I told him about my family, and he told me some more about his. The conversation was refreshing because we took a step back from where we'd started the first day he answered the phone and learned a lot more about each other. After spending some quality time in the park, he took me back home. He walked me up to my door and kissed me on the cheek.

"Oh, you're not going to come in?" I asked.

"No, not this time." He laughed.

"Call me later?"

"Okay."

Tyree got back into his truck. He blew me a kiss as he drove off. I thought that was sweet. I went back in the house and called Joi, but her machine came on, so I left a message. I decided to take it slow for the rest of the day and wait for Tyree to call. I did a load of laundry and rearranged my closet. Around 8:00 p.m., my telephone started to ring. As I checked the caller ID, I realize that it was Joi calling, not Tyree.

"Hello, Joi."

"Did Tyree call you back?" she asked, skipping the small talk.

"Yes, he did. Hold on, Joi. I have another call, and I need to click over." I switched to the other line. "Hello?"

"Hey! How's my baby doing?"

"Tyree? Hold on." I clicked back to the other line. "Joi, I have to call you back. Tyree is on the other line."

"Well, excuse me. Go handle your business, and call me later," said Joi.

Chapter 8

Stalker

Joi

Wow. I hadn't realized that I was staring into space for what seemed like an eternity until my computer announced, "You've got mail."

I had broken my neck to see if Jaylen had sent me an e-mail, but there was nothing there from him. Jaylen and I had shared so many years of happiness and love. Now, it just seemed as though it had happened a lifetime ago. As I checked my e-mails, I noticed that I had a shit-load of forwards from all over the place. That was it. I was going to e-mail everyone who had sent these e-mails, which consisted of inspirational messages and chain letters; forward this and that for good luck, along with money schemes, jokes, and so forth; and tell them to remove me from their forward list. Now I was being added to e-mail lists of people I didn't know who had taken my name from another list.

There were a couple of e-mails from Damon. One read: Long time, no hear from. What does a brotha got to do to get a call and let me know that you're okay? Another one read: Roses are red, violets are blue, and I bet you'll never guess who's been watching you. Smile. I didn't even respond to his messages. He was really starting to work my nerves. He must have forgotten that I was an attorney, and that I would legally dig all up his ass. He would be shitting out restraining orders.

I met him at the law firm where I was an intern. He was seeking legal advice from one of the attorneys/sports agents at the firm in regards to his career. As I was making my way back to my desk, he introduced himself.

"Hi. I'm Damon," he said as he extended his hand out to shake mine.

"Hi. My name is Joi," I said, with a shy smile.

"Are you an attorney?" he asked.

"Yes, I am."

"May I ask what area of law you specialize in?"

"Criminal law," I told him.

We seemed to hit it off immediately. We went out for lunch that same day. I was not going to front; I was a little starstruck. Damon was a number one pick in the first round and played for the Philadelphia Eagles. As we got to know each other some more, he invited me to his home. His home was like something out of *Cribs* or a beautiful homes magazine. I was so caught up in what he represented that I overlooked the obvious. After the relationship became more serious, I realized that I was not prepared for his kind of lifestyle. Sometimes I didn't see him for weeks at a time, because he traveled throughout the season. I went to all of his home games and to a few away ones. When he was home during the off-season, he was just as busy, if not more so, as he was when he was playing. I was so devastated by my breakup with Jaylen that dating a professional athlete seemed to be just the excitement I needed to help me get over it.

However, this lifestyle had its ups and downs. The groupies were everywhere you looked. I assumed he had other women on the side, so I made it a point not to get completely caught up. I just let the chips fall where they needed to. Eventually, the relationship started dwindling, and every now and then, he would call and accuse me of cheating on him when he was away. This was his way of trying to balance out his own guilt. He had a lot of nerve checking up on me. Shit, game recognized game. Eventually, I just defined it, or us, as friends with benefits. It was what it was.

Damon had a degree in communications; however, football was his life. It devastated him when he found out that he had developed a tumor in one of his shoulders after he was injured during a game. He was forced to retire from the NFL. He was able to get a position as a commentator with a local TV sports station. He loved his job, but he just did not get the notoriety that he'd enjoyed while playing in the NFL. He needed that attention, and if you ignored him, he couldn't handle it. He wanted his women to sweat him and stay all up under him, but I just didn't get down like that. He was a straight-up pain in the ass. I even went as far as putting the song on my answering machine in hopes that he would get the message. No! I needed my space. And he was just a half-assed substitute for the one and only love of my life.

Ring . . . ring.

"Hello?"

"What's up, Joi?"

"Oh, hi, Damon," I said, sounding somewhat disappointed that he'd called.

"Don't get too excited. I figured that I would call you since you don't seem to want to call me. You're not even responding to my e-mails," he said in a sarcastic tone.

"Look, Damon. I really don't appreciate most of your e-mails."

"Why? All I did was throw a little poetry up in 'em."

"No. They sounded more like stalker material," I said flatly.

"I know you're not callin' me a stalker. Shit, you ain't all that. I've dated model chicks that would make you look stupid."

"Look, Damon. I could care less who you used to date and who you date now, because you are a has-been, and you have been for a while. Besides, those model chicks are not thinking about you."

"Joi, you're just a stuck-up, bitter bitch," he snarled.

"You know what, Damon? I normally would respond, but I'm not. You're not worth it. I just want you to stop calling me and sending me e-mails. That's all I want you to do."

"Cool. I won't call or e-mail you. But I guarantee you this. You'll need me before I need you," he growled.

"Are you finished, Damon? Because I really need to go."

"A'ight. I'm out. Peace."

I could hear him mumble "Bitch" before he put the phone down. I hoped he was pissed off enough to leave me the hell alone. If I didn't ever hear from Damon again, it would be *too soon*. If I happened to see him on TV, I would just change the channel. I wasn't feeling him like that anymore. I was so done and he was so beat.

"Poof, be gone," I said and laughed to myself.

Hmm. It felt like a huge weight had just been lifted off of me. I was two seconds from changing my e-mail address and phone numbers. I just hoped he was serious. If I knew he would leave me the hell alone, I would go and pay for a so-called model chick to date him. But it was so difficult when you had a profession that required you to carry yourself in a particular way, one that was conducive to the acceptable ways of society. I had to be a pillar of the community. There was no room for ghetto. You just had to know when to shift gears. There was a time and place for everything. You couldn't always keep it real. I needed to calm down, because Damon was working my nerves. *Let me call my girls to see what's up,* I thought.

Ring . . . ring.

"Hey, Taj. Hold on. Let me get Eboni on a two-way," I said.

"What's up, Joi?" said Eboni.

"Hold on, Eboni. Let me click over to Taj." I switched to the other line. "Is everybody on?" I asked.

"Yeah, we're on, Joi. What's up?" said Taj.

"Y'all want to go out next weekend? I heard Floetry and Erykah Badu are going to be in town, at the Munsey Theatre. After the show, we can go to the club!" I said.

"Girls' night out?" asked Taj.

"Most definitely. What about Faith? I'll call her after we hang up," I replied.

"Please, she's in love. She ain't even tryin' to go nowhere unless it is with Tyree," Eboni said.

"There is no such word as *ain't.* You are so ignorant at times," Taj replied.

"Who cares, Taj? You know what the hell I mean, don't cha?" Eboni retorted.

"Screw Tyree. She can go out one night with us," I said.

"That's probably just what she will do. Screw Tyree," said Taj.

Everybody just laughed through the phone.

"Oops, my bad. I forgot to ask Lex. She's been going through a little something, but I know she'll come," I said.

After we hung up, I realized that what it all boiled down to was that we all needed a night out. Taj and Eboni needed to find a man. I, hopefully, had just got rid of one, but I wanted my old one back. Besides, my boss had dumped some more cases from our other office on my desk because the attorney working on them was in the hospital indefinitely. Faith was strung out over some guy named Tyree, who she had just met, and Lex's husband was cheating on Lex with some big, fat, obnoxious chick. What was he thinking? My telephone rang seconds before I called Lex and Faith.

"Hello?" I said.

"What's up, baby girl?"

"What, Damon?"

"Oh, it's like that? We have one little fight on the phone, and you are ready to trade me in like a used car."

"Look, Damon. I don't have time for your bullshit. We said what we had to say, so just leave me alone."

"I'm not ready to leave you alone. I can't just flick my emotions on and off like a light switch. I love you, baby girl."

"What? What's love got to do with anything? We're not even like that anymore. Please stop calling me!" I shouted.

"Can't we sit down and talk about this like two grown-ass adults?"

"No, Damon, we cannot. I have to go," I replied, hanging up.

I needed to take a nap. I was tired and overworked. I decided to snuggle up in my chair for some brief shut-eye. Ten minutes into my nap, the telephone rang.

"Ha-lo," I said, half asleep.

"Hi, Joi. It's me, Lex. Wake up. I need to talk."

"About what, and can it wait for at least two hours?" I asked.

"Not really."

"Okay, Auntie Alexis. What could be so important that it can't wait for another hour and fifty-eight minutes?"

"Nothing . . . ," she said, laughing.

All I could do was laugh back because she was half crazy.

"Look, Lex. I got Damon harassing me, and now you. What's up with that? Are you two in cahoots?"

"What's he been doing?"

"He's been calling me, watching me, arguing over nothing, hanging up, and then calling back, saying, 'I love you.'"

"Joi, something is seriously wrong with him. You need to stay clear of his psycho ass. I'm serious. He does not sound too stable," Lex warned.

"Girl, you don't have to tell me twice. I do watch *Forensic Files* and *America's Most Wanted*."

"Have you ever been to his house?"

"Yup. It's very nice. He has the dual staircase in his foyer. They are perfect when your man pisses you the hell off and you go to the left and he goes to the right. He has a gourmet kitchen with the granite countertops and stainless-steel appliances. He has a four-car garage, inground pool with swim-up bars, theater room. You know designer this and designer that."

"That's probably the home he wants you to see. I bet you he has one of those little psycho houses that sits up on the hill off of a back road, and he and his dead mother rent out the rooms and then kill the customers."

"Shit, he might. I wouldn't put it past him," I said.

We both laughed at that one.

"No, for real, Joi. You're not only my niece, but you're my girl, and I don't know what I would do if something were to happen to you."

"I hear you, Lex. The feeling is mutual."

"I'm just saying that I know you know how to basically take care of yourself, but you really need to zero in on this one and handle your business. I mean, get a restraining order."

"I really do not want to publicize my business like that. It's embarrassing," I said.

"Well, do something before it's too late."

"Well, for your information, Lex, I hired a private investigator to do some checking around. He's a good friend of mine, so when he gets back to me, I'll get back to you."

"Okay, Miss Thang, you'd better, or else," Lex said.

"Or else what?" I asked.

"I'm going to tell my older sister, who happens to be your mother the last time I checked."

"Okay, Lex. Enough about me. How are you doing?"

"I'm hanging in there. I missed a couple of days of work. I had an upset stomach, so I couldn't keep anything down."

"You're probably just stressing. How's everything with Craig?" I asked.

"You know, I'm dealing. Sometimes he comes home, and then other times, I don't see him for a couple of days. I refuse to keep arguing about it. I'm just trying to save some money so that my son and I can get the heck out of here."

"Well, you and Brandon are always welcome to come and stay with me until you get things straightened out," I said.

"I know, and I thank you, but no thanks."

"Why did you say 'Thanks, but no thanks'?"

"Because you're being stalked by a crazy man, so we're not going to be stalked with you," she said, laughing cautiously.

"Oh. Before we hang up, Lex, all the girls are getting together to go and see Floetry and Erykah Badu. You down?"

"Yeah, count me in. I need to keep myself active so that I can stay focused on other things."

"Okay, I will let you know all the details when I get them. I'll call you later. Bye."

"Bye."

Ring . . . ring.

Who is it now? I thought.

I scurried to the phone to answer before whoever was calling hung up.

"Hello," I said.

"Bitter bitch!" *Click.*

I could not believe it. His whole demeanor was crazy. I seriously needed to put an end to this entire situation with Damon.

Chapter 9

Monday
Morning Blues

Joi, four months later . . .

I just didn't do Mondays well. Hell, I didn't do any days well that had to do with work. So now here I was, years later, a criminal attorney. It was Monday, and my desk was piled high with criminal cases out the ying-yang; I had to go to court later this afternoon, and I was not mentally ready; my office was too cold; and my boss kept ringing my telephone.

"This is Joi speaking."

"I need to see you in my office."

Dammit! I thought. That was all I needed first thing in the morning—a call from the boss, especially an overbearing, pain in the ass, micromanaging control freak. I could see that the red lights on my telephone were all lit up, and I couldn't even get a chance to deal with them before this unexpected meeting.

I went in to my boss's office and sat down, and he went on and on with his petty bullshit. Sometimes I just thought his sole purpose in life was to make me miserable because he needed a life. For a second, I wanted to tell his ass to stop calling me, trying to control my cases, and then blaming me for his fucked-up decisions. I did not go to law school for this bullshit. *Call your own number or somebody else, and leave me the hell alone,* I thought.

That was what I wanted to say, but he was being transferred within a month, so I dealt with it. It just could not get any worse. I was actually working with Osama bin Laden. No wonder they couldn't find his ass. He was working with me, blowing up my phone, my computer, my departments, my mornings, my nights, and my weekends. Damn, he just basically blew up my mind. I couldn't wait for this meeting to be over. After the first fifteen minutes, his words just faded, anyway.

Just leave, motherfucker. Leave, I said to myself over and over again.

I made my way back to my office to grab my coffee mug and then headed to the break room. I fixed my coffee and finally sat down to sort out my work for the day. My personal assistant had been out all week with the flu, and everything was piling up. Realizing that I had not checked my messages, I picked up the telephone to see who had called.

Beep! "This is Kim. I won't be in today—feeling sick."

Beep! "This is Mr. Korzack from Burcek Inc., and I need for someone at the firm to return my call today."

Beep! "Joi, this is Jaylen. When you get this message, please give me a call. Bye."

What! He sounded a little upset. Ooh . . . Let me call him right now. I could care less if the senior partner of this law firm called me right about now; this was one call I was going to make without any interruptions. I didn't want to appear desperate, but I was. This crazy rush just came over me. *What does he want?* I thought. It had been every bit of at least four months since the wedding, and now he'd decided to call me.

"Okay, Joi. Calm down," I told myself. I grabbed my hands and took a deep breath. I kept telling myself, "You can do this, girl!"

I didn't know exactly how to explain what I was feeling, but I felt like crying. This one message had dragged up so many old emotions that I had to get myself together. I was nervous, mad, and confused. I kept remembering the wedding and the fact that he'd been crying.

Fuck you, Jaylen! I yelled inside.

I kept playing out the conversation inside of my head. The nice version went a little something like this.

Hi! How's everything? Good, good . . . How's the wifey? I know the honeymoon was nice . . . ha-ha! It's so good to hear from ya! The wedding was delightful. . . .

That was not going to work. He knew me too well, and he would know I was being fake. Okay. I would try the hurt and wounded version.

Hi. Just returning your call. What do you mean, it sounds like I have an attitude? I don't have an attitude. Well, at least I wasn't crying at my wedding. Crybaby! "I can't believe I'm so mean and bitter," I said, pounding my hand.

My state of mind wouldn't allow me to return his call just then. I was better than that, and I refused to play myself out. I'd call in five minutes. Shit, he was on my time. I was just going to call him, and no matter what, I would be supportive and happy for him.

I finally dialed the number.

"Hello. This is Jaylen."

"Hey, Jay. This is Joi, returning your call."

"What's up, girl? I was just calling to check on you and chat a little. Did you enjoy yourself at the wedding?" he asked.

"Everything was really, really nice," I said.

"Okay, tell me how you really feel."

"I don't know what you are talking about, Jaylen."

"Joi, you seemed like something was bothering you. I asked you to dance, and you kept pulling away from me, saying no."

"I was just tired," I lied.

"Well, I'm glad I was finally able to convince you to dance with me."

"Me too. I had fun. So, how was your honeymoon?"

"It was really nice. We went on a cruise to the Bahamas and . . ." I just tuned him out like a broken TV. He had a lot of nerve giving me detail after detail, with the exception of one thing. I had to cut him off on the real.

"So, how many times did you fuck her, and is she pregnant?" I asked.

"Damn, Joi! Is it like that?"

"Yes, Jay, it's like that." I knew I had stepped over the line, and that my questions were so inappropriate. I had no right to come at him like that, but it was too late now. "I'm sorry, Jay. I was out of line. I don't know what came over me. So, how's the wifey? You know, I had a dream that you were going to call me and tell me that she was pregnant."

"Well, now that you mention it, we are expecting."

All I knew was that I felt my lips moving to respond, but the words were not coming out. *Somebody get me some oxygen before I pass out,* I thought. Then, without further hesitation and losing what dignity I had left, I asked him, "How could you do this to me? To us?" *Uh-oh. I'm losing control of myself.* I was truly bugging. Whatever I was feeling at the wedding had been tripled by this news.

"Joi, please calm down. I really didn't want to

tell you, but I felt I owed you that much. I did not want you to find out from somebody else. Believe me, my intentions are not to hurt you."

"So, how many months is she?"

"She's four months pregnant," he replied.

"I guess she got pregnant on the honeymoon."

"Not exactly. It kind of happened before the wedding."

"So, are you guys excited?" I asked.

"Well, I'm excited."

"What does that mean?"

He told me that Toni really did not want any children, because her career was so demanding, and that she'd told him that she got pregnant only because she felt like he was pressuring her.

"I still can't believe she would say that to you. Having a baby is a blessing and should be something exciting that you both share," I said. "Well, did you two discuss this before you decided to have a baby?"

"Joi, you know that I have always wanted a son or daughter of my own. I just want a family, and you know that if it's a boy, he will definitely wrestle, run track, or play football."

"You still didn't answer my question. Did you two discuss this prior to your getting married and her getting pregnant?"

"Not directly. We just talked about having a family, and I just assumed we were on the same page," he confessed.

"So, to make a long story short, the pregnancy was unplanned?" I asked.

"Pretty much, since you put it that way."

He went on to tell me some of the things that had happened on their honeymoon. She had kept disappearing while they were on the cruise. Apparently, Toni had been up to something, and Jaylen needed to get to the bottom of this. Who in the hell was this mystery man named K. J.? Why had he always been conveniently in the vicinity of Jaylen and Toni? Where had his damn wife been? There were way too many unanswered questions. He said that one minute they were arguing, and the next minute, they were fine. Hmm, maybe Toni was bipolar.

She had also communicated to him that she had not even wanted to have a big wedding. She had only done it because that was what he had wanted. He hadn't had a choice. He had to have a big wedding because he had a large family and knew so many people.

"I don't like what I'm hearing, Jay. Those comments had to be very hurtful to you," I said.

"Well, all I know is that since she got pregnant, all she's done is complain and sleep. I know that she is pregnant, but she acts like she is crippled. She stopped working because she supposedly doesn't want to expose the baby, because she is around computers all day. I come home, clean the house, cook, do laundry and yard work. Do you think that she is so grouchy and moody because she is pregnant?"

"Maybe, Jay. Maybe. I've never been pregnant, so I can't answer you," I replied. "Just sit her down and really see where her head is at regarding your marriage and the baby. Just keep working on it. Put it in God's hands. You'll be fine."

What else could I say? This was a good man, and I had let him get away. I wanted so badly to dog out his wife, but realistically, I knew that it took two. I understood what he was saying, but I could not offer him the advice he needed. I had to tell him to work on it, because I might be in her shoes one day. He seemed to be so down, and I had to step back and respect his space. As bad as I wanted him back, I didn't want him while he was in this state of mind. I knew I had to love him from a distance, and it was very difficult. I also knew that he needed me, which made me feel good. He trusted me as his friend, and I wanted him to be happy with or without me.

"You really need to talk this over with her. You shouldn't be going through this in the first four months of your marriage," I said.

"She won't listen. I try to sit her down and explain where I'm coming from, and she just blows it off. I mean, she never wants to talk about it. I don't mean to bog you down with all of this. I'm just realizing my mistakes."

"No, you just didn't take the time to get to know her. Think about it. Don't you know me inside and out?"

"Yes," he replied.

"You know my favorite color, my favorite food, my favorite show, and so forth. We like the same kind of music and shopping for art. We went to college together, lived together, and hung out together. We have mutual friends, and we're close to each other's family. We've been there for each other through good and bad times. You know what makes me happy and what makes me sad."

"You're right," he said quietly.

It was hard trying to get him to open up a little more. I knew I'd hurt him years ago, but I had been stupid. Deep down inside, part of me felt for him. The other part wanted him back in my life . . . for good. I figured that if he felt the need to call me, then I was feeling the need to know. *Let's put it all out on the table.*

"Jay, I'm not trying to be all up in your business, but I was not feeling her at your wedding. She wasn't smiling, and she wrote down your wedding vows on a piece of paper. Yeah, I said it. I'm sorry if it sounds harsh, but I had to say it."

"Well, don't hold back," he said.

"Since you mentioned not holding back, I can't believe your ass was up there crying, making me feel like our relationship wasn't all what I thought it was."

"Joi, it's not like that. I was caught up in the joy of the event. But it's not like I was boo-hooing."

"You might as well have been. My girls were straight clowning the situation. I know that they were questioning the relationship we had and assuming that it wasn't all it was cracked up to be according to those tears rolling down your face. How could you?"

"Girl, why are you trippin'?"

"I'm so sorry, Jay. I thought I could handle this, but I can't. I would not be myself if I bottled my true feelings inside. Your wedding devastated me. It was the hardest thing I've ever had to witness in my life. She doesn't deserve you. I should have been the woman walking down that aisle, saying my vows from the heart, on the real."

"So, what would you have said?" he asked.

"Jaylen, for as long as I've known you, from the moment I laid eyes on you, I've loved you. I never thought in a million years I could find someone who could brighten my world, my spirit, and my heart. I promise to cherish each and every moment with you, and to share a family and a loving relationship. I promise you that I will always be by your side through the good and bad times. My heart skips a beat whenever I see you or hear your voice. When we are apart, I carry the love I feel for you with me everywhere I go. Mentally, you stay on my mind twenty-four hours a day; emotionally, you are my rock; and physically, you far exceed all my needs. I truly believe that we are soul mates, and I could not have been blessed with a better person to share my life with, because you complete me," I said tearfully.

"Baby, don't cry," he said.

"I can't help it. I messed up, and I'm messed up. I'm sitting here in my office, boo-hooing over a married man whom I'm so deeply in love with, it frightens me."

"I love you, too, Joi. I'm not just saying this because you're crying. I mean every last word of it.

I did try to replace you. I thought we would spend the rest our lives together and grow old side by side. You accepted my proposal, and then you turned around and accepted that job in Newark, New Jersey. I couldn't compete with that, and why should I? I knew that you loved me, but you also loved your career. I could have relocated with you, expanded my firm, but I let my pride and the influence of others make my decision. I was taught that to be a man, you need to handle your business and make decisions that are beneficial. We could have worked this out."

"So, where do we go from here?" I asked.

"Well, I plan to take care of my child, and if that means on a part-time basis, so be it. I don't want to split my family up, but I need to be happy, too. I've talked to my pastor at the church, my family, and her family, and they want us to work it out. But why should I, Joi? I would only be prolonging the inevitable. Who's to say that in five years things will change? That would only make it more difficult to leave. I need to cut my losses now, take care of my child, and get on with my life. She went and purchased this enormous house without consulting me first. She just figures that I am going to spend up all my money while she just sits back. I told her that a larger house is not going to solve our problems. Who wants to live in a house that's not a home?"

"What money are you talking about? You got some extra money that I don't know about?"

"It's a long story. I'll fill you in later."

Chapter 10

Reflections

Joi

From the first day I saw him, I knew my life would never be the same. I was returning to college for my sophomore year at Cheyney University. I met Jaylen at the gym in college. He was sitting there, wearing a white T-shirt and some black shorts, waiting to play basketball. He signaled with his finger for me to come over, so I went to see what he wanted.

"Are you a freshman?" he asked.

"No, I am a sophomore."

"Well, I'm also a sophomore, but I've never seen you around campus."

"Well, I've never seen you, either."

"So what's your name?" he asked.

"Joi Nicole," I responded.

"Is your last name Nicole?" he asked, smiling.

"No, it is my middle name. I just like the way it sounds," I said, smiling back.

"So, do you have a boyfriend, Joi Nicole?"

"You sure ask a lot of questions, and I have no idea what your name is."

"Jaylen."

"Well, it's nice to meet you, Jaylen, and by the way, I do have a boyfriend," I told him.

"So does he go here, or is he tucked away at home somewhere?"

"Home, if you must know."

"Tell your boyfriend that I'm going to take you away from him," he asserted.

"I doubt it."

I walked away, smiling to myself, and then out of nowhere my roommate, Eboni, appeared.

"Joi, did that guy try to talk to you?" she asked.

"Uh, sorta, kinda," I hedged.

"Well, he looks like a keeper. So if you don't want him, can I have him?"

The last thing I needed was another brotha hittin' on me at college. However, I just didn't want Eboni to know how instantly attracted I was to him. It could be tough at a predominately black college—you know, too many fine black men everywhere you go. How did you separate the good ones from the bad? Some were quite the gentlemen, while others acted like immature boys in men's clothing. Some of them roamed through the dormitories, uninvited, and it just got on my nerves. At other times, you could meet someone who could sweep you right off your feet.

I was interested, but I had a boyfriend back home. I wondered if I was trying to convince myself that that relationship was serious.

One day I managed to be a sweetheart for a fraternity, and they had us selling carnations for Valentine's Day. I had to hand deliver carnations from secret admirers to the different dormitories. Out of nowhere my girl Taj bum-rushed me.

"Joi, who's Jaylen?" Taj asked.

"I don't know. Why?" I said.

"Well, he is sending you some carnations. I started reading the order form and saw your name, so I had to make a detour from my route and find you."

"Stop, girl. Let me see the order form." It read: *To Joi, someone I would like to get to know better. Happy Valentine's Day. P.S. Remember what I told you at the gym.* It quickly dawned on me. It was the guy from the gym.

How sweet, I thought.

Nobody had ever sent me flowers before. I just felt so obligated to go across the street to the mall, buy him a card, and have the college mailman place it in his campus mailbox. I made it a point to run to the mall and buy him a card for Valentine's Day. The card was pretty basic. It read: *Someone nice to remember on Valentine's Day.* I had to admit he had piqued my interest. I went to my other girlfriend Adell's room, and out of nowhere she told me that her cousin, a guy, wanted her to get me over to her room while he was there.

"Who's your cousin?" I asked.

"You know him already," she said.

"Do I? What's his name?" I quizzed.

"His name is Jaylen," she said.

"Get out of here. Girl, he sent me some carnations. Adell, I look a mess. I have to go."

"Joi, please don't leave yet. He literally begged me to get you over there."

"You never told me you had relatives on campus," I said.

"Girl, please. I introduced you to him before. You just forgot."

"Well, how long is he going to be here? Because I'm going to a fraternity skating party. Let me go and get dressed. I will come back in half an hour."

I went back to my room and told my roommate, Eboni. She was happy for me. "Girl, let me know if he has any brothers. If so, holla at your girl," she said.

Eboni and I headed to Adell's room and knocked. "Come in," Adell said.

I walked in, and there he was. He was fine. *Damn*. He was tall, brown, and handsome, with the cutest dimples I had ever seen in my life.

Is this the same brotha I met at the gym? What am I thinking? I wondered. I got so nervous that I asked Adell for a drink. She grabbed a beer from her refrigerator and passed it to me. He had the audacity to frown at me. It was obvious he did not drink, but I was not going to let his nonalcoholic ass affect me. I mean, I thought he was cute, but he just didn't know me well enough to be judging me. We talked for a minute, while my roommate sat quietly in the corner, looking as if her world had crumbled. Then Eboni and I left and went skating, and he stayed there and waited for me to return. After visiting hours, he left and called me on the telephone, and we talked all night. I told him what Eboni had said and asked him if he had a brother that he could introduce her to. He responded by saying he had a brother, but his brother had a girlfriend, and it was a serious relationship.

Over the next several weeks, he sent me card after card after card. He said that he felt like he was falling in love with me, and I was feeling the same way. I remembered the first time we kissed. I had received a page in the lobby of my dorm. "Joi, you have a visitor in the lobby," the dorm assistant had announced over the intercom.

I knew it was Jaylen, so I went downstairs to sign him in, and it seemed like all the girls who knew me in the dorm, especially the single ones, were hanging out in the lobby. It was so obvious that they were being nosy. Anyway, we went back to my room. I cooked some cheeseburgers on my hot plate and some Oodles of Noodles. He claimed he had already eaten and wasn't hungry, so I just helped myself. We talked about our family, friends, and college life. I could tell he had his head on straight. Jaylen had his life mapped out from *A* to *Z*. Afterwards, I started switching the channels on the television, and one of my favorite movies of all time was on— *The Color Purple*.

After the movie was over, Jaylen and I talked some more, and he asked me for a kiss. He was somewhat nervous during the first kiss, so I had to pull him back into the room for another one. He kept acting like he was shy, but I knew it was an act, because he hadn't acted shy at the gym. It was so obvious that we were attracted to each other. Eventually, we started spending so much time together that it was hard to go home on the weekends. We both still had some unfinished business we needed to handle. I had a soon-to-be ex-boyfriend back home, and Jaylen had a very recent ex-girlfriend.

He was so nice. He would send cards to my house if he knew I was going home on the weekend. The card would arrive on Saturday, saying that he missed me and that he loved me. Whenever I came back to campus, he would be waiting for me by my dorm, ready to take my luggage to my room. He would take the last couple of dollars he'd earned from work-study and treat me to the movies at the mall. One time it had been raining, and the grass was wet. He gave me a piggyback ride so that my shoes would not get wet. He was so thoughtful and genuinely nice. To top it off, he had the nicest clothes and lots of them. I never saw him wear the same thing twice. He would walk me back to my dorm every night, unless he was visiting me. It took me a while to sleep with him, because I did not want to rush it and then lose it.

After a while, we both decided it was time to take the relationship to another level. At last, our first intimate experience. He played Luther Vandross's song "Superstar/Until You Come Back to Me." Whew. I still remember those words. We started off by kissing and holding each other, and then everything took its course. It was the most romantic night of my life. He definitely had it going on that night. I knew that I was definitely in love from that moment on. We skipped a few classes here and there just so that we could be together. Through the course of the relationship, we definitely experienced our share of ups and downs. Although we both lived in New Jersey, we were from different towns. We had to rely on the train and the bus to see each other because I didn't have a car, and neither did Jay. The odds always seemed to be against us. But we made the best of it. He would call me every night, all summer, whenever we could not be together. He never missed a night. I mean, *never.* I still had all his cards and letters tucked away.

We finally graduated from college. I was able to get a temp job at a student-loan company, filing and answering the telephones. It was not exactly what I had had in mind, but I needed some money, and it was a mile from my parents' house. I had always wanted to be an attorney, but I needed a break from school. I decided that

I would enjoy the summer and focus on law school in the fall. I had already met Jaylen's parents, and he already knew mine. My mom and dad loved Jaylen like he was their own son, and I had a good relationship with his family. My motivation for wanting to go to law school had a lot to do with my brother, Wil. I wanted to make a difference, and I knew my brother would have been proud.

In the fall, I studied for the LSAT exam and scored high. After submitting many applications, I was finally accepted to the Howard University School of Law. I would just go to school, study, and come home to New Jersey every other weekend. After three years of studying, I graduated at the top of my class. Afterwards, I had to take another break to study for the bar. I was so overwhelmed, but I knew I had to pass the first time. Failure was not an option for me. I joined a study group and got myself a tutor. At last, I passed the bar.

My parents, along with Jaylen, threw me a surprise celebration, and things seemed to be going great. I eventually accepted a position in Freehold, New Jersey, to clerk for one of the meanest judges on the East Coast. He obviously watched way too many judicial sitcoms on television. Most attorneys already had a bad reputation, and my goal was to be the exception to the rule. I wanted to help people and give back any way I could. The only thing I talked about to Jay was work. I could tell he was getting a little annoyed, and I accused him of not supporting me. By this time, it was obvious that the commute to my new job was definitely taking its toll and hurting the relationship. Jaylen felt as though I was putting everything into my job and leaving nothing for him. I promised him that I would focus more time and energy on us as soon as I could balance my schedule.

Finally, he suggested that we move in together. I told him yes and resigned from my job. My parents were not crazy about the idea, but they respected my decision. Many people often reminded me of a famous quote: "Why buy the cow when the milk is free?" You couldn't tell me anything, though. I had it all figured out. I was an attorney, the first one in my family; I knew it all. I constantly told myself that Jaylen and I would live together, get to know each other more, and take it from there. I had convinced myself that I was going to get to know my mate first to avoid any potential matrimonial disasters.

After an extensive job search, I received a call from the prosecutor's office in Newark, New Jersey. The only problem was the distance, once again. They wanted to set up an interview right away. I agreed and met with them the following week. Jaylen appeared to be happy for me, yet unsure as to how this would affect our relationship. I returned home, not knowing whether or not they were really interested. I had a lot to think about. I sent a thank-you letter to the office the next day. Two weeks went by and still nothing. I figured that I would move on to plan B and go down to the public defenders' office to see if my services were needed. I accepted a position at the public defenders' office to make ends meet and build my résumé.

Things were going good, and Jaylen asked me to marry him. I accepted his proposal, and we set a date for the following September. As fate would have it, I was offered a position with the prosecutor's office in Newark, New Jersey. This was a job I so desperately wanted. The salary was not that great, but I wasn't doing it primarily for the money. I wanted to make a difference and hold people accountable for crimes they committed, among other things. They told me to think about it for a couple of days and get back to them because they needed to fill this position.

I told Jay about it that same day, and after discussing the pros and cons, our wedding plans, and yet another long-distance relationship, it was obvious that he was not feeling it. He just had so much pride. He insisted that I take the job because he did not want to stand in my way. Jaylen did not quite understand why I would accept a low-paying job. It was clear to me that he did not understand why I became an attorney. I tried to explain to Jaylen what this opportunity meant to me and how important it was. It was not about the money. He said he understood, but I doubted it. Besides, he had his own investment firm and could not just hop up and leave at the drop of a dime.

He also made it crystal clear that he would not wait for me forever.

I did not know how to take that. I didn't know if we were a couple or not. I prayed about it and cried about it. I stepped out on faith and accepted the job, anyway. Again, I knew it all. I had it figured out. I would ask Jaylen to relocate to Newark, New Jersey, and help him open another investment firm. We could move in together and get married. Voilà! This was the only way, and besides, we could not handle the pressure of not seeing each other, constant travel on both our parts, and conflicting careers. Eventually, we just drifted apart.

Chapter 11

Head Games

Faith

I got up this morning, thinking about Tyree. I checked my answering machine in hopes that he had left me a message while I was asleep. "You have no new messages," the machine announced. I slowly walked over to the refrigerator to pour myself some orange juice.

Tyree had not been himself for several weeks now. Every time I thought we were getting closer, he pulled away. We'd been to the movies and out to dinner a few times, but I'd never been to his house, which was strange, because he'd been to my house.

Maybe he's pulling away because I told him that I loved him on our first date. No wonder he's acting distant. I probably scared him off. I finally told myself that I would call him by noon if I did not hear from him first. *At least I haven't given up the booty yet,* I thought.

I couldn't even wait until noon. I dialed his number at 11:55 on the nose. *Ring . . . ring. Click, click.* "Hey, this is Tyree. Holla at cha later. Peace."

"Hi, Tyree. This is Faith. Give me a call."

All of a sudden I felt nervous, and my stomach was doing flip-flops. I had all these emotions going on at the same time. Was it really love? Or was it just loneliness? Who knew? I wanted to call him again, but only fifteen minutes had passed. *Maybe he just checked his messages, and he'll call me back in a few minutes,* I thought. Just as I picked up my glass of orange juice, the phone rang and my heart jumped. I looked at my caller ID, and it read RESTRICTED. I quickly regrouped and tried to pretend that I wasn't pressed, and then I calmly answered the phone.

"Hello. This is Faith."

"Hey, boo. Sorry I didn't call you sooner. I passed out last night, and this morning I went to the gym."

Before I could respond in a way that would let him know that I was pissed, he asked me out again. Shit. I was so happy, I just dropped the whole entire subject.

"So, where are we going?" I asked.

"To a nice, mature club. I haven't danced in a while, so this might be the perfect time to go. I figured we could do something a little different than dinner and a movie. Besides, I want to show my girl off. So make sure you wear something sexy. Not too much. Just enough to leave something to the imagination. I got to go. Just be ready at nine tonight. I'll come by and scoop you up."

I hung up the phone and threw my hands in the air. "Yes! It's going to be on tonight."

I found an outfit to fit the occasion. Not too much, not too little. I decided to wear a pink Baby Phat V-necked, multicolored halter top. I put on a black, asymmetrical skirt with some soft pink, high-heeled sling-backs. My beautician had put some flips in my hair, and my make-up was flawless. Finally, I was ready for the night. I was looking cute and sexy. I kneeled on my couch so that I could look out the window until he arrived. Nine o'clock passed, 9:30 passed, and no Tyree. I called his number, got his machine, and left a message.

"Tyree, this is Faith. I've been here waiting for you since nine. Please call me and let me know what you're going to do, or if something came up."

I decided to get a blanket and lie down on the couch. I wanted to be able to hear his knock or his horn when he came. I dozed off and woke up throughout the night. I looked at the clock for the last time, and it said 3:47 a.m. I was hoping that he would have at least called while I was asleep, but there were no messages and no new calls on my caller ID. I was devastated. I finally fell off to sleep again in spite of tossing and turning. Strike one!

I got up the next morning, pissed! *Who does this trifling asshole think he is? But that's cool, because I do not have time for the bullshit. When he calls, if he calls, I am going to just tell him to leave me the hell alone,* I thought angrily.

That was why I tried to tell myself not to get all excited over a brotha, because when they let you down, you felt like you hit rock bottom.

Why can't I just find someone who truly cares about me? I thought. *I'm so tired of being by myself or hooking up with a man who only wants us to be friends with benefits. It's okay to have a good job, a nice home, and a car, but it's even better when you have someone to share it with.*

I felt as if I was about to break down. I told myself to get it together, so I did. *I'm not going to let this inconsiderate, selfish boy break me down. If he doesn't see me for who I am, well, that's his loss,* I told myself.

I decided to work out. I threw on some gym gear and ran around the park. I saw a couple of cuties, but I decided to stay focused. I came back home and jumped into the shower. I figured that I would just throw on some jeans and a T-shirt since I had no plans for the day. I fed the fish in my mini aquarium and watered my plants. I then grabbed a book I had been reading and lay down on the couch.

Around 10:30 a.m., the telephone rang. I tripped over the cord as I reached for the phone.

"Hello?" I said, breathing heavily.

"What's up, shawty?" he blurted out.

"Who's calling?" I asked.

I knew who in the hell it was, but I figured I would feed him a little of the bullshit back.

"It's me, Tyree. You already forgot my voice? Isn't this some bullshit," he said.

"I don't know. You tell me," I replied sarcastically.

"What's wrong now? What did I do?" he asked.

I can't believe he is acting like he didn't stand me up last night!

"Well, since you want to play little games, I'll humor you. Let's see, Tyree. What happened to our little date last night? Or did something or someone else come up?"

"Look, Faith, I apologize about last night. I'm going through something crazy in my life right now, and I don't know how to handle it. Can we talk about this in person? I have something I need to explain to you."

"I don't know, Tyree. It might be better to cut our losses and move on." Deep down inside, I wanted to see him so bad and listen to his bullshit explanation.

"Please, Faith. Just give me a chance to explain," he pleaded.

"Well, how come you need to come all the way over here to explain? Start explaining over the phone."

"No, I need to discuss this with you face-to-face."

"Okay, only for a few. I'm kind of busy today."

"I can respect that. I'll be there in thirty minutes."

"Why don't I just come to your place for a change?"

"Baby, that's not necessary, because I'm on my way out the door right now. I don't want to inconvenience you any more than I have already."

"Well, if you're not, I will be walking out of my door in thirty minutes and two seconds flat, because I have things to do," I warned.

We hung up, and I took off running to the bedroom to change my clothes and fix my hair. I put on my next best outfit in the closet, sprayed perfume all over, and put on some make-up. I wanted him to see and smell what he'd been missing. I had also planned to walk out the door right behind him when he left. I wanted him to feel a certain kind of way about it. I was only going to go to the car wash and then come right back home.

He has exactly fifteen minutes to get here, or I'm out. I wonder what he needs to talk to me about. I started feeling like I had hundreds of butterflies in my stomach. His car pulled up five minutes later. I grabbed my keys and ran out the door. I did not want to be alone in the house with him, because one thing would just lead to another. I wanted to get to the bottom of this, with no distractions. As I walked toward his truck, he pushed open the passenger door for me to get in. I felt him staring at me so hard, I couldn't even look back at him.

"How come you won't look at me?" he asked.

"I don't know." I put my head down.

He then gently took my hand and turned my face toward him, and I turned away. I felt so weird. I wanted to relax, but I didn't want to let my guard down. He needed to know that he just couldn't treat me like I was nothing.

"Please, look at me, Faith."

Finally he started up his truck and drove off. A few minutes later, his cell phone buzzed. He reached for his cell, looked at the text message, and put it down. I wanted to ask him so bad who it was that had called, but it wasn't my place. I was just jealous. The cell buzzed again. He picked it up again and then shook his head in frustration as he ignored the text message for the second time. I just couldn't resist it anymore.

"Who's blowing up your cell phone?" I asked.

"Just my ex. She's trippin'," Tyree said, as if he didn't know what to say.

"Trippin' over what?"

He acted as though he did not hear me and continued to drive to the movie theater parking lot.

I asked him again. "Trippin' over what, Tyree? Just tell me the truth. What's going on with you?"

He then proceeded to put on his Musiq Soulchild CD. "Just listen to these three songs for a few minutes."

The first song he played was saying, "Mary, how could you go? . . . I've tried so hard to please you, baby." The next song was saying, "One, four, three—and that means I love you," and then finally "Love" came on. He seemed so intense when the part came on that said, "Through all the ups and downs." I just looked at him until the song went off.

"Now that you finished gettin' your groove on, I'd appreciate it if you would enlighten me with whatever is on your mind," I said.

"Well, it's like this. I used to deal with this girl named Cre'ole for about a year, and I recently told her that I did not want to be with her anymore."

"Why?" I asked.

"Because she's crazy. I never planned to make her my woman, because of the way I met her."

"And what way is that?" I asked

"That's not important right now," he responded. "Anyway, she keeps calling me, crying and shit. She calls me all day."

"Does she live near you?"

"No, she lives about an hour away, but she has some relatives that live near me. She makes it a point to come down and visit them just so she can figure out a way to come over. To top everything off, she just told me that she's pregnant. I'm not ready for kids right now." His cell buzzed. "That's her again," he said.

"Just call her back and see what she wants. It won't bother me," I lied.

He decided to ignore the call. As soon as he put his cell phone away, she was ringing it again.

Stalker? I thought to myself.

"Hello! Cre', what do you want?" he barked.

I could see he was getting upset, and I could hear a female voice screaming, crying, and shouting through the phone. He then held the phone up in the air. I could hear her say things like "Why are you treating me like this? I love you, and you said that you would always be there for me . . . I'm going to kill myself."

Oh shit. This female is buggin', I thought to myself.

He then looked at the phone, shook his head, and put it away.

"Tyree, she said that she was going to kill herself," I pointed out.

"I know, but that's how she tries to hold on. I remember one time she tried to jump out of my truck when I was driving her back home. We used to argue and fight all the time, and I just made a decision to end the relationship because the shit was embarrassing."

Bzzzz, Bzzzz. I peeped over to read his text message. It said to call home right away. *Home?* I thought. *I could have sworn he told me that she did not live with him. What have I gotten myself into?*

He was so stressed out that he didn't even notice that I had read the message. Strike two!

He then picked up his cell phone and dialed a number. It was obvious that it was her again. She was screaming even louder now. "I know you're out fucking somebody else!" she screamed through the phone.

"Look, I said I'll be there in a few, so stop fuckin' calling me!!" Tyree yelled.

He hung up again and slammed his hand on the steering wheel. We sat in complete silence for about ten minutes. I just stared out the window.

"I'm sorry that you had to hear that, but that's my story. I don't know how to get out of this relationship," he conceded. "She told me that she would kill herself before she would let go. I'm scared. I don't want that on my conscience. That's the real reason why I never showed up. We got into an argument, and she just started crying and threatening me that she would call the police and say that I hit her if I tried to go out. I couldn't even call you."

I just sat there thinking for a few minutes. Then I took a deep breath and said, "I know that you have a lot on your plate, and right now I want to be there for you, but this is a lot to absorb. I just need a little time."

"Well, I'll understand if this is too much for you to handle. I don't want to lose you. I feel so comfortable around you. Out of all the women I've dated, you're different. I want a companion who is my best friend, as well as my lover. Though I've only known you for a short while, I can tell you're the one I'd like to explore that opportunity with."

Whatever. He's probably feeding me bullshit, I thought to myself.

He drove me back home. I kissed him and told him to go handle his business.

"I'll call you later," he said as I closed the passenger door.

I went inside and poured myself some wine, because that was a horrible date. I checked my machine, and the first message was from Tina. "Hey, Faith. I was calling to chat and see if you would be interested in going on a retreat with my church next month. It's going to be nice. I'll fill you in later."

Beep. "What's up, Faith? This is Joi. Where are you? Call me tonight."

I lay down on the couch. *I probably should go on the retreat, because this relationship is stressing me out already,* I thought. *I'll call Tina and Joi both back later.* I was numb. I didn't know what to think. I had a million things running through my head. *Does this female live with him? Is he married? Does he beat her up? I mean, arguing is one thing, but he said fighting. Is he a dog? A ho? Does he really care about me?* The questions went on and on. I just refused to let this brotha consume my every waking and sleeping moment.

I needed to get myself together. I had told all my girlfriends and my family about this man I'd met. I'd bragged about his looks, bangin' body, independence, nice truck, and good job. I had told them how respectful and caring he was with me. Now I was going to look like a damn fool. I tried to convince myself that because we had never been physically intimate, I wouldn't miss what I had never had. Yeah, right.

There was no way I wasn't going to get with

him. Besides, as crazy as it sounded, his crazy ex-girlfriend, and soon-to-be baby's momma, or whatever you call her, had only confirmed that he had it going on in the bedroom. Nobody trips that hard over just any man. I wanted so very much to be that best friend and lover he had claimed he wanted in me, but damn he had major drama. I needed to call my best friend, Joi, for some advice.

Chapter 12

The Storm

Joi

Ring. Ring. Click.

"Hey, Joi. Where are you?" Lex asked.

"I've been in a car accident," I replied, sounding frustrated.

"What happened?" she asked.

"Some idiot ran the light and hit the tail end of my car while I was coming from another direction."

"Are you okay?"

"Yes, I'm fine," I assured her.

"Where are you at?" Lex asked.

"I am in the emergency room, waiting for the doctor to release me."

"What hospital are you at?" she asked.

"I'm at Central Shore Medical Center."

"All you had to say was that you didn't want to pick me up today. You did not have to go and get into an accident. I finally caught a ride home after an hour had passed. I refused to stay at my job another second. Who's coming to get you?" Lex asked.

"I don't know. I tried to call my parents' home, but nobody answered."

"I'm on my way up there to pick you up. You're going to make me miss the Soul Train Music Awards, but that's okay," Lex said, laughing on the phone.

"Do you have the car?" I asked.

"Yes, I do. I took those keys from Craig the minute he got home from work."

"Okay. I'll be waiting."

I had to subject myself to the whole ambulance scene just in case I needed to sue the person who had hit me. But when you were an attorney, you just tried not to go there. It was an easy five thousand minimum with a verbal threshold. Still, unless all your bones were broken or you were half dead, it was difficult to sue. The doctor had asked me where it hurt and told me to touch my toes. It was actually killing me to bend over. I had to request a CAT scan because I really had a bad headache. The entire process was so time consuming, but I was in pain and needed to get checked.

Finally, my Mom, Dad, and Aunt Alexis all arrived at the hospital.

"Lex, do you feel all right? You look like you don't feel well," I said.

"I do feel a little sick, Joi. I might go to the doctor and make sure it's not my kidney again," Lex replied.

My mom and dad signed me out, and then we went home. I stayed home from work for two weeks. My doctor felt it was for the best. I did not need for him to tell me that. I was well overdue for a serious break. I still was dragging those extra cases around with me. I wanted so bad to call Jaylen and tell him about my accident, but I couldn't. I just really wanted to hear his voice and see how he was doing. Damon continued to call and hang up and play his little games. He had issues. I couldn't wait to talk to the private investigator I had hired.

I arrived at work at 8:15 a.m., and what seemed mentally like an hour later was only 8:25 a.m. on the clock. This first day back at work seemed to drag on and on. Aunt Alexis left me a message to remind me to pick her up from work. She had been catching the bus while I was recuperating because Craig had been taking the car. I could not wait until 5:00 p.m. arrived. Eventually, my time was up, and I grabbed my briefcase, literally ran out of the building, jumped into my car, blasted the music, and sung my heart out until I got to Aunt Alexis's job. She worked as a cashier at a clothing store at the local mall. I parked my car right in front of the door and waited. All of a sudden, this little, frail woman walked up to my car.

Whoa! It was Lex. She looked sick and weak.

"Lex? How much weight did you lose?" I asked, with concern.

"I really don't know, Joi. But I do need to get to the doctor."

"I thought you were going two weeks ago."

"Girl, neither Craig nor I have benefits, and I just did not have the money," she explained.

"I would have given you the money to go. You cannot play with your health."

Lex had always been petite, but she looked every bit ninety-five pounds, soaking wet. I was really concerned about her.

"Have you been taking your medicine?"

"Sometimes," she said.

"What do you mean by *sometimes*?"

"Joi, I don't have benefits, and my medicine costs about five hundred a month. I barely make that in a month's time. I go to the pharmacy and ask for five or ten dollars worth of medicine. I tell them two of these, one of those."

I could not believe what I was hearing. "Lex, how is it that the pharmacy is allowing you to break up your medication like that? Isn't that unethical?"

"Oh Lord, I forgot who I was talking to. The pharmacist knows Craig, and he is just hooking me up until I figure something out."

"Well, he should have figured out a way to fill

your entire prescription," I said. "What good is your medicine doing if you are not taking the required dosage? Are you able to get some assistance with your medication?"

"I tried, but they said we make too much money. We bring in only forty thousand dollars a year combined."

"Alexis, I know you're too proud, but you should have let the family know so that we could help you."

"I did not want to bother anybody. Everyone has bills and their own families to take care of. I did not want to be a burden. I'm okay, though."

"No, you're not!" I said in disbelief.

I knew Lex was proud and private to some extent, but this was her life, and I was so mad at her. I dropped her off at her apartment and drove home. I called my mother and told her about Lex. She contacted the rest of the family to let them know. Without hesitation, we all decided to assist her financially. I was going to the pharmacy to get all her medication the next morning.

However, that same night, my uncle James, Aunt Mary, and Alexis's husband ended up taking Lex to the emergency room. My mother called me and told me that the doctors wanted to admit her to make sure her kidneys were functioning properly.

I told myself, *Okay, we've been down this road before. She'll pull through. Oh, Lord, please take care of Lex. She's been through so much.* I continued to pray until I fell asleep. I tossed all night, anyway.

My mother worked at the hospital. Hell, 50 percent of my relatives worked there, including me at one point, before I went off to college. The next day I figured that I would call and check on my auntie around noon. I was stressing at work all morning, but what else was new? I called my mother at her job.

"Hi, Mom. What's up? What are the doctors saying?" I asked.

"Well, they are still running some tests," she replied, with a worried tone.

"Please keep me posted," I said.

I knew something was just not right. Lex looked so weak and frail. The next afternoon, I went up to the hospital to visit her.

"Hey, Aunt Alexis. How are you feeling?" I asked as I gave her a kiss on her forehead.

"I feel a little better. It's probably my kidney acting up again. They are still running tests. I should know something this week," Lex said.

I stayed with her for a couple of hours, then left. On my way out, I bumped into Mom and Aunt Mary, who was a registered nurse, and they really looked worried.

"What's wrong?" I asked.

"Well, the doctors ran some tests, and they seem to think that Lex may have cancer. They want to do a biopsy tomorrow. If it is cancer, they are going to have to perform surgery immediately to try to keep it from spreading," Aunt Mary said.

"Does she know?" I asked.

"Yes, she does, but she doesn't know that we know it might be cancer," Mom informed me.

Apparently, my aunt Mary had picked up Lex's son, Brandon, from the hospital, and he had asked her what cancer was. My aunt wanted to know why he was asking, so he told her that the doctors had come into the room to tell his mother they thought she might have cancer and that they needed to do some kind of test in the morning. He was young and did not completely understand. Aunt Mary panicked and read Lex's chart and confirmed the inevitable. She called my mother and the rest of the immediate family. Lex did not want anyone to know, especially my mother, because she did not want us to worry. She would have held on to this secret until it became obvious. I knew that my mom was taking this hard, because my grandmother had died from ovarian cancer when she was only forty-one years old. Now, Lex, her baby sister, was going through the same thing, and she was only thirty-five. From that point on, my mind just shut down.

"Please, God, don't let her die. She has a little boy and a husband," I cried.

My mom hugged me, and we cried until we could not cry anymore. I finally got myself together and convinced myself that it was just her kidney, not cancer. We went home and made the necessary calls. I didn't sleep all night.

The next day, I called out from work and went straight to the hospital.

"Good morning, Auntie. What's up?" I said as I walked into Lex's room.

"I just want to get out of here. I want to go to the movies, but I'm stuck here in the hospital," Lex moaned.

"Did the doctors say anything yet?" I asked, already knowing the answer.

"Well, they said my kidney might be acting up again. They also told me that they did not think it was anything like cancer, but I had my biopsy today to make sure everything's okay."

It was tearing all of us apart inside. Lex obviously did not want me to worry. I just looked at her. I could not even imagine the slightest possibility of losing her, ever! I was unusually quiet. I could tell she knew I was not myself. I just told her that I had had a long night and was tired.

"I need a perm," Lex said.

"I'll put a perm in your hair, but how can I get your head over to the sink if you can barely walk?" I asked.

"Ask the nurse to get you a geri chair, and I can lay my head back," Lex responded.

"Okay. I'll run to the store and pick up a perm. I'll be right back."

I went to the store, bought a perm, and came back to the hospital. The nurse helped me put Lex into the geri chair. I pulled her hair back into a ponytail after I permed it. It was the best I could do under the circumstances. Afterwards, I styled her hair and put a little make-up on her face.

"Joi, I have cancer," Lex blurted out of nowhere.

It felt like somebody had punched me in my stomach. I managed to pull myself together in an effort to respond to her comment.

"You're going to be fine. You have to." Then I reached over and hugged her so tight, and we both started to cry. "Lex, I'm so sorry. I'm so sorry, but you got to beat this. God is so good. You have to just have faith."

"They said I have to go to radiation, chemotherapy, and dialysis."

"All three?" I asked.

"Yeah, because the tumor is pressing down on my kidney, which is causing some problems, so I have to go back on dialysis."

"I'll go with you to your treatments today."

"Well, I only have radiation treatments today. They should be up here in a few to get me."

"How come you didn't tell the family? You know we all would be here for you," I said.

"I know. I didn't want to worry anybody. I guess the rest of the family already knows?" Lex asked.

"Maybe," I said quietly. "Do you need me to do anything?"

"No, I'm just worried about Brandon right now. I want to see him graduate from the fifth grade. My marriage is on the rocks. I don't know how serious my illness is. I'm craving lobster and may never get the chance to eat one."

"Girl, the last thing you need to be worrying about is some lobster. Everything is going to be just fine." We both managed to laugh.

"If I do get the chance, I'm going to go to a restaurant and eat me one," Lex added.

"I'll get you one, Lex." I could tell she wanted to change the subject, so we did.

Transportation finally arrived to take her down to radiation. I hopped on the elevator with them. It took a while for her treatment to be completed, but I stayed in the waiting room. I was glad I could be there with her. We went back to her room, and I lay down next to her in the hospital bed. I knew she was scared, so I stayed until her husband showed up.

"Hi, Craig," I said softly when he entered the room.

"Hey, Niecy," he responded tearfully.

He gave me a hug and sat down as I was leaving. I could tell that he was scared. He had this look on his face like his world was crumbling. As messed up as things were between them, I knew he loved her. He was just screwin' up his marriage. I did not want to complicate things, so I told myself that I would try to separate the two issues. Her health was our family's main concern.

As I went down the elevator, I bumped into Craig's mother and my cousin Amelia. They asked me how Lex was doing. I told them that she was in good spirits. I gave them all hugs and left the hospital. I had planned to go to Jamaica for a vacation in May, but I wasn't sure how things were going to play out with Lex being sick. If her condition worsened, I would definitely cancel the trip. Besides, I would not enjoy myself.

As time passed, Lex's room grew into a florist shop, her hair began to fall out, and she lost about another twenty pounds. The doctors said it was alopecia, which was temporary hair loss. Lex said that when she finally got home, she was going to go to the barbershop and chop all her hair off. I was trying to go shopping for bathing suits and short sets for my trip to Jamaica, and it was crazy. How could I be going to a tropical island to have fun when my best friend, Aunt Alexis, was dealing with a life-threatening ordeal? Needless to say, I barely ate, which led me to lose almost twenty pounds my damn self. I looked like I was on crack. I did, however, manage to go to the health-food store to buy some weight gain supplements.

It was apparent that Lex's condition was not improving, but the doctors decided to let her go home for a few days. All of the immediate family came up to the hospital to move flower arrangements, balloons, and plants to help her husband and son with the transfer. I wanted to call Lex at home, but since she had just arrived, I decided to give them some space.

Damn. My trip is in a couple of weeks. What am I going to do? I just can't go. I don't want to leave her like this, I silently told myself. I made myself go and lie down before I called to check on her. I couldn't help thinking about all that she was going through. Here she was sick, and her husband was having an affair.

"She doesn't deserve this," I cried over and over again. "Please, Lord, all she wants is to see her son graduate from fifth grade. Please give her that," I prayed and prayed.

Lex and her son had a great relationship. He was her life. She'd been told that she could never have children, that it would kill her, but she had wanted a baby so bad. So, she'd risked her life to bring one into this world. He was the cutest little boy you'd ever want to see. They would ride their bikes together, walk to the store together, and just spend quality time together all the time. She loved him with every breath in her body. He was her ring bearer in her and Craig's wedding. Brandon loved his mother, too. He had so much respect and admiration for her. They shared a bond that nobody could ever tear apart.

Anyway, I finally fell asleep and woke up around 6:00 p.m. I quickly dialed Craig and Lex's house.

"Hello, Craig. This is Joi. How's Aunt Lex?"

"She's okay. Mary, James, and Amelia took her to the barbershop to get her hair cut."

"What?" I said.

"Niecy, you know how headstrong she is. All she kept asking us to do was to take her to the barbershop. I stayed here with Brandon, because he knows something is wrong with his mother, but he just does not understand everything," Craig said.

I suddenly felt a false sense of hope. I figured that since she was able to go to the barbershop, she might be able to go with me to the movies or something. I got into my car and drove over to my parents' house. For the first time in weeks, I sat down and stuffed my face. Mom and Dad told me that the family was going to take turns helping out. Well, I planned on going over to Lex's tomorrow after work.

The next day after work, I drove over to Lex's apartment to help out.

"Hey, Lex! I'm so glad you're home. Do you think the doctor will let you go to the movies or to the park?" I asked.

"Girl, not with my ass hurting like this," she said.

I could tell she wasn't 100 percent. What was I talking about? She wasn't even 50 percent. It looked like she probably needed to go back into the hospital.

"Brandon, what are you doing?" Lex yelled.

"Mom, I'm cooking you some hamburger meat, like you asked me to," Brandon responded.

"You know I can't eat a hamburger from frozen hamburger meat. It just doesn't come out right if you put it into the microwave! Dammit! Can't you do anything right?" she yelled back.

Brandon looked shocked, yet okay. He knew that this was not his mother's normal character.

His father took him into the bedroom and explained to him that his mother was not feeling well. Lex and Craig had decided that they would sit down real soon and explain everything to him. He seemed to understand. I could tell Lex was getting frustrated, so I tried to cheer her up by talking about something else. After a while, her apartment became crowded, so I left and went home to my parents'. Later that evening, my aunt Mary called, crying and upset.

"What's wrong, Aunt Mary?" I asked.

Taking a deep breath, she said, "I stopped by Lex's tonight, and when I got to the door, I heard all of this screaming and crying. I quickly opened the door and asked what was going on in there."

"So what happened?" I asked.

"Lex had just told Craig and Brandon that she was dying, and she was letting them know who she wanted to raise Brandon and making final arrangements. I slammed the door, jumped in my car, and cried all the way home. I just couldn't handle it."

I began sniffling, and then we both started crying together on the phone. My mom came and took the phone. She wanted to know what was wrong. I told her, and she broke down like I'd never seen her do before. This was her baby sister, and she felt helpless. My dad came downstairs, hung up the telephone, and consoled us until we were able to get ourselves together.

The next day, I received a call from Craig. He said that Lex had been admitted back into the hospital. From that point on, everything seemed to go downhill. She was on chemotherapy, radiation, and dialysis just about every day. And she was in so much pain. There were times when the hospital would leave her screaming outside of the dialysis room, bleeding. The family was constantly battling with the hospital administration. It was taking its toll on everybody. Every time I spoke to someone in the family, we usually ended up in tears. We were strong, but this was just so hard, and we still constantly prayed for a miracle. Now Lex weighed about seventy-five pounds. I didn't know if she would make it past Mother's Day.

Lex made it perfectly clear that she did not want anyone crying in her room, or they would be asked to leave. I would just walk down the hall and cry because it was so hard. No matter how strong she was, it was still hard. I admired her so much because she put our feelings first, in spite of her situation. She never felt sorry for herself or asked why. She was a trooper through it all. I knew her so well. I knew it bothered her when her husband was not at the hospital. It wasn't hard to figure out that he was with Elisha. Lex needed him so bad. I hated him, and I hated Elisha. She worked in the place where her lover's wife lay sick, fighting cancer. She didn't even have the decency to respect their marriage or herself, especially now.

A few days later, Gi'ana, Eboni, Faith, Tina, and I went to the hospital to visit Lex, and she put on her best act of pretending that she was feeling better. Tina held her hand and prayed for about fifteen minutes. Taj was too upset to come to the hospital. It tripped us out that Lex's hospital roommate was also suffering from some type of cancer. She had no breasts, and her husband was just stretched out at her feet. We were so nervous and sad at the same time. Lex's roommate died the next day. When Lex told me about it, I knew she was really scared.

The following week, I took my mother to Red Lobster for Mother's Day. I knew that she needed a break, and she loved to go to that restaurant. The host escorted us to our seats, and as we turned the corner, I caught a glimpse of a couple resembling Craig and Elisha. I sat with my back facing them. I was so pissed off, and my mother was so hurt.

"I know this black motherfucker didn't bring his fat bitch to Red Lobster on Mother's Day while his wife is lying in the hospital, dying!" I yelled across the table. "I'm going to go over there and say something."

"Joi, please, please, don't go over there and say anything. Please, do that for me. I'll talk to him about this," Mom said, pleading with me.

I hit the table with my fist, and I could feel the tears rolling down my face. I was so mad, and if they knew like I knew, they would already be on the highway. I finally calmed down enough to get myself together, but I was no longer hungry. I had lost my appetite. However, I decided to turn around in my chair and stare them down. After about five minutes of my staring at them, they finally left. Craig couldn't even look over at us. My mother ordered herself something to eat. I wanted to get Alexis a lobster, but she was on a strict hospital diet.

I was so upset that I could hardly drive home afterward.

"Mom, I'm so sorry I ruined your Mother's Day dinner, but how could he do this to her?" I said, sobbing as I drove.

"I know, baby," Mom said.

"She is going through so much, and all he is doing is disrespecting her while she lies up in the hospital in constant pain. It's not fair. She doesn't deserve this. I love her so much, and she is dying, Mom. Lex is dying. What are we going to do? What about Brandon? He needs her so much. Oh, God, she's only thirty-five years old. What can we do to help her? I feel so helpless."

I pulled over until I got myself together. I had literally fallen apart. This was way too much to handle. Mom just cried the whole way home. I gave her a long hug and told her that everything was going to be all right.

The whole situation continued to take its toll on the entire family. I reached out to Jaylen; I wanted him to know because he loved Alexis, too. I left a message on his machine and asked him to call me back.

Lex's condition was especially taking a toll on my cousin Amelia. She and Lex had shared a room as they were growing up, and she truly looked up to her as her older sister, and not only as an aunt. We always talked about it with each other to get us both through.

The next time I went into Lex's room, there was this weird silence, and she was breathing extra hard. I was afraid to wake her up because I knew she was in a lot of pain and on morphine. So, I picked up the Bible and read to her while she was sleeping. I wanted to stay with her, whether she realized it or not.

"Hey, Joi," she said faintly.

"Hi, Lex. Go back to sleep. You're tired."

"How long have you been here?" Lex asked.

"For about an hour."

"I want you to know, in case I don't get a chance to say good-bye, that I love you," Lex said.

"I love you, too, Aunt Lex. Please, you're not going anywhere."

"I know my time is near," Lex said.

"Please don't say that." It took everything inside me not to cry, so I just choked on my tears. All we could do was put it in God's hands at this point. I didn't know how much time she had left, but I knew her time was near. The nurse came in and gave her some more medication. Soon she fell asleep again. I kissed her forehead and told her once again, "I love you. Good night."

Chapter 13

Girlz Night Out

Joi

Well, I should have known. Taj and Eboni had pulled a fast one. Here I was supposed to be getting ready for the Erykah Badu and Floetry concert, and they got Faith and me to go with their horny asses to a sex-toy party. Those two really needed a man. Maybe this was what I needed. Here Lex was, fighting for her life, and I was out trying to have some fun. I guessed all of us needed to get out. Faith was strung out over some guy named Tyree, who was taking her through a lot of bullshit with his psycho supposedly ex-girlfriend, and I was being stalked by a nut.

I pulled up into this new development with upscale homes. I could see Taj's, Eboni's, and

Faith's cars parked throughout the block. I found the house where the party was being held, walked up to the door, and knocked.

"Come in!" someone yelled.

"Hi," I said, smiling in a shy sort of way.

"Find yourself a seat and enjoy the presentation. There's food and drinks in the other room. Please help yourself," the hostess said.

There were at least thirty-five to forty women in all colors, shapes, and sizes, and of all ages. I grabbed a cup of spiked punch with marinated fruit and sat down next to a Caucasian woman.

"Ladies, today, I'm going to show and tell you how to please yourself and your partner," said the woman doing the presentation. "There are too many of us out here who are faking orgasms. You should be fed up! Get yours! Because you know after he gets his, his ass is somewhere snoring. Anyway, how many of us have difficulty reaching an orgasm?"

I looked around because I did not want to be the only one raising my hand. Then I saw about seven women raise their hands, so I hesitantly raised mine also.

"To the ladies who did *not* raise their hands, most of you are lying to yourself. Trust me. I will show you some products that will help you reach that ultimate orgasm," said the woman.

"Let us see some toys!" somebody yelled.

The woman doing the presentation started passing around all kinds of pink, purple, and green vibrators with little faces. There was also a toy there that you could place around your man's penis, and it would flicker at your clitoris when you were having sex. I was starting to feel tipsy and hungry, but I was truly amazed by some of these toys. I then saw the woman lift this huge, twelve- or fourteen-inch chocolate dildo in the air.

"Ladies, next we have the Chocolate Thunder, and yes, the myth *is* true," she said.

I leaned over to the Caucasian woman sitting next to me and said, "The myth is not always true."

"Oh, girlfriend, please! I've dated a lot of black men, and, boy, do I know," she replied.

"I'm just trying to keep it real. Hmm, forget Chocolate Thunder. It might be Chocolate Wonder," I said, laughing.

By now, I was truly, truly tipsy, and I was very, very hungry. I got up and made myself a plate of food, and I stayed in the kitchen until I was done.

"I'm never going to make it to the show tonight if I don't get at least three hours of sleep," I said to myself.

It was two in the afternoon, and the show started at eight. I would need to leave here by three, be asleep by three thirty, get up at six thirty, shower, get dressed, and leave by seven thirty so that I would arrive a little before eight. Finally, everybody was starting to order some toys and leave. The line was so long. I grabbed a cup of coffee to help sober myself up while I was waiting. I just could not believe all the sexually deprived freaks up in here. I guessed I was one, too. Anyway, I finally placed my order. I just figured that I would help the hostess out. Got it?

Eighty-one dollars? I silently yelled at myself. I wasn't that damn horny. Everybody was whipping out credit cards, cash, checks, and change. I paid for my order, and they gave me my bag with another order form for future reference.

"I don't think so," I said while peeking in my bag.

I looked around for Taj, Faith, and Eboni. They were all over in the corner, laughing and talking as if they had just purchased some men. They had that look that said, "It's going to be on tonight." Knowing my girls, they might drop it like it was hot with their new toys.

"Hey, Joi. What did you buy?" Taj asked.

"None ya," I replied.

"Girl, please. We are all grown-ups in here. I'm not going to think any different of your prissy ass," Taj retorted.

"Your mother," I said.

We all just started laughing, but I still was not going to let her nosy behind peek in my bag.

"Well, I'm getting ready to leave. I'm tired, and I need to lie down before the show," I said.

"Eboni and Taj, are y'all bringing those bags with you tonight?" Faith asked.

"Now why would we do something stupid like that?" Eboni asked.

"Oh, my bad. I thought the bags were your new men!" Faith replied, laughing.

"I know Faith did not go there," I said, chuckling to myself.

"I'm just playing. I just needed a little laughy. I'm sorry. You all know that you all are my girls for life," said Faith.

Eboni and Taj vowed to get her ass back.

"So, Joi, what are you wearing tonight?" Faith asked.

"Some big pants, clogs, and Afro puffs," I said.

"Yeah, right," said Taj.

"I am," I insisted. "I want to vibe with them. I heard that the people come to their concerts in all kinds of tricked-up gear. You have to have that look."

"What look?" Taj asked.

"Shit, I don't know. Dress the way you want. Who cares?" I said.

"Well, I'm out. I will meet you guys at our spot at seven thirty so we can drive together," Faith said.

We finally got into our vehicles and headed home. It took me only about fifteen minutes to get there. I set my clock for six thirty and literally jumped into bed.

Bzzz, bzzz.

I looked up, and the clock said 6:30 p.m. It felt like I had just fallen asleep ten minutes ago. I managed to get up and immediately jumped into the shower. After I got out, I wrapped a towel around my body and sat down on the edge of my bed. Anyway, I put on my Floetry CD to take my mind off of things. Then I put on my bell-bottom jeans, which had a matching jacket, my brown clogs, a chocolate brown turtleneck, and the jacket. I pulled my hair back into two pigtails and attached some Afro puffs to each one. I sat down in front of my vanity mirror and proceeded to put on my make-up. Finally, I sprayed on some Still by J-Lo and found some nice earrings that really accentuated my gear. At least, I thought I looked nice.

Ring . . . ring . . .

"Hello?"

"Hey, Joi. I have Taj and Eboni on the telephone with me. Are you ready? Because we're getting ready to meet up at the spot."

"Yes, Faith, I'm ready. I'll see you there in ten minutes or less. Bye."

"Peace."

We all met at the spot; then they all hopped into my ride. Taj, Eboni, and Faith looked so fly that I started feeling out of place.

"Joi, girl, we thought your outfit was going to be kind of crazy, but you hooked it up. I mean, seriously, you did the damn thing. I am feelin' that," Faith said, sounding impressed.

Now I felt better. I paid them back some compliments. I loved my girlfriends like they were extra sisters. I drove off and ran smack-dab into traffic. The traffic started moving about five minutes later. We finally arrived at the concert, but parking was at least two blocks away. After I parked the car in the lot, we ran most of the way because the show was about to start.

Once we got inside, there were people everywhere. They were selling T-shirts, food, ice cream, popcorn, beer, and soda. There were Afros, Afro puffs, dreadlocks, straight weaves, braids, and so forth. Basically, people wore a little bit of everything. We purchased some food and drinks. Then the usher escorted us to our seats, which were in the middle, so the people in the end seats had to get up and let us through. They looked frustrated, but so what.

Some unknown group was performing when we sat down. They put their thing down, but I did not have a clue who they were, and I was not pressed about finding out, either. Floetry came out next and rocked it. They sounded better than the CD, so I was definitely feelin' that. I would definitely go see them again. There was a fifteen-minute intermission after they walked off. The people started setting up for the main attraction—Erykah Badu. We all got up to go to the ladies' room and freshen up. Everyone seemed to be enjoying themselves except Faith. I could tell. She was over in the corner, talking to Tyree. She was moving her hands and covering her face while she talked, as if she was trying to explain something.

Mmm, I thought to myself.

When the show was about to start, we anxiously sat and waited for Erykah Badu, and finally she made her entrance. The crowd, which was sold out, went crazy. The first song she sang was "Puff," and 75 percent of the people stood up, including me, and started jammin' off the

Chapter 14

Strike Three!

Faith

It had been a whole week, and I still had not heard from this Negro. I wanted to call him something else, but I just didn't like that word. But that was what I got. I had allowed my loneliness to dictate who I would allow to mistreat me and take me for granted. I mean, I loved him, and I missed him, yet I couldn't stand him. I wanted to be in a relationship, but not this bad. But was I willing to give it up? I mean, we had some unfinished business. I hadn't even slept with him yet. I guessed it didn't matter, because fuckin' somebody who did not care about me or respect me would only make me feel horrible. I just didn't do the empty sex thing. You might as well be in a relationship with your vibrator. It didn't care and neither did he. It couldn't hug you, talk to you, or call you, and neither did he. I was just confused. Well, I needed to bring some closure to this iffy relationship. The bottom line was that he needed to return my call, and I knew exactly how to get his attention. So I dialed his number.

Ring, Ring. Click, click. "Hey, this is Tyree. You know what to do. Peace."

"Hey, Tyree. It's Faith again. Look, call me when you get a chance. Some female called my cell phone, and she was asking me a lot of questions about you. Okay, bye."

I bet he will call me back like Johnny-on-the-spot, I thought. Shit, it wasn't even two minutes, and my phone was ringing. It was him.

"Hey, beautiful," he said.

I really couldn't believe this asshole. He must have really thought I was stupid. Not that I was not beautiful, but how could he just not call me all week and then call me "beautiful," like everything was hunky-dory?

"What's up, Mr. Tyree?"

"Oh, I'm Mr. Tyree now, huh?"

"Mr. or Mrs. What difference does it make?" I said.

"Because I'm a man, not a woman."

"I couldn't tell. Hmm, every time Cre' says jump, you act like a little bitch and jump."

"Faith, please stop trippin'. You know I had things that I had to take care of. That's why I didn't call you for a couple of days."

"A couple of days? Why don't you try a week? But that's okay because you have to make a decision before I make one for you. I'm not for your constant bullshit. I'm clever! Do you hear me? Contrary to what you might think, I'm not stupid. All you had to do was be honest."

"Come on, Faith. I'm doing the best I can," he replied.

"Well, your best is at its worst right about now, and it has been for a while. You barely call, and we really don't do anything with each other."

"Babe, I told you that my ex is crazy."

"I'm not trying to hear this. Because if everything that you said was true, then your ass is crazy, too," I yelled.

"Look, Faith, I promise you that I will stop over later on tonight, and we can talk about this," he said calmly.

"I'm not going to be home. You wish I would just sit around waiting for you. You have truly lost your mind. Besides, I have plans."

"Then I'll come by tomorrow morning. I almost forgot that tonight would not have been good, because I have to do something for my mother. Okay. Well, I have to hang up now. Peace."

"Why do I put up with his ass?" I sighed. "He ain't even worth it. Shit, it's not like I have a lot invested in him," I said, talking to myself.

I needed to get away and clear my head. What I needed to do was call Tina and RSVP on that retreat. I decided to call her now before I changed my mind.

Ring . . . ring.

"Hello?"

"Hey, Tina. This is Faith. I was calling to see if I could reserve a space for the retreat next week."

"Girl, it's not a problem. I'll put your name down on the list."

"So what's it about?" I asked.

"What's what about?"

"The retreat."

"Oh, it's so nice and refreshing. You get to focus on yourself. No radios and no TVs. There are a lot of powerful seminars by some extraordinary women. I can go on and on. Believe you me, you will come back feeling like a new person."

"That's what I need right about now."

"Well, Faith, I will drop off a brochure that will explain everything."

"Thanks, Tina," I said.

"No, thank you. I'm so excited you're coming."

"Okay, I'll see you later. Bye."

A retreat sounded really good, but I needed some immediate relief. I needed to call Joi and see if she wanted to go out for a drink and listen to some poetry. I knew that I was in the mood to hear some. Who knew? I might grab the mic tonight. I had heard Dat Baw Dave was going to be there. I just loved his poetry. My favorite was "Can I Be That Friend?" The females seemed to go crazy over that one, and it didn't hurt that he was also a hottie. If he pointed me out on that one tonight, I just didn't know what I would do.

Ring . . . ring.

"Hi, this is Joi. Please leave a message." *Beep! Let me try her on her cell,* I thought.

Ring . . . ring.

"Hello," Joi said.

"Hey, Joi. I really need for you to do me a favor tonight."

"What is it? Because I have a lot of work to do tonight."

"Ooooh, please. I need for you to come with me to open mic tonight," I said.

"I don't know, Faith. I just got dumped on with all these unsolved criminal cases. My feet hurt. I'm hungry, and I'm tired."

"Dat Baw Dave is going to be there," I informed her.

"Tonight?"

"Yeah, tonight."

"Ooh, count me in," she said.

"I thought that you were so out of it. 'I'm busy. I'm tired. My feet hurt. I'm hungry,'" I said in a whiny voice.

"Just come and pick me up, Faith. I'll be ready."

"Okay, I'll be there around seven p.m."

Well, that was settled. I knew Joi would come with me once she heard Dat Baw Dave was going to be there. He was her favorite poet. Hmm, he was my favorite, too. There was no need for me to sit around waiting for Tyree to call me. Besides, he'd claimed that he had to do something with his mother. He just didn't know a good woman when he saw one, but hey, that was his loss. One day, he'd wake up, but it would be too late. I was going to find myself a doctor. Right now, I'm horny, and Tyree was not even around to finally hit it.

Later that night at the club . . .

Joi and I walked in the club, and it was semi-crowded. We located a small table with two seats and sat down. The lights were dim, and there were a few amateur poets trying to put their thing down. I loved poetry with meaning, but that militant, combative shit had to go. It sounded like they were yelling at you or reciting it in 3-D. It was not even necessary. I wanted to just tell them to bring it down. The bartender came over and took our orders. Dat Baw Dave was not due to come on until later.

"So, Faith, you gonna get on the mic?" Joi asked.

"I'm not sure yet. If I start feeling it, then I'll get up there. A true poet just goes with the flow," I explained.

Laughing, Joi asked, "So, have you heard from Tyree?"

"Yeah."

"How come you didn't ask him to come?"

"Because he has to do something for his mother. You know how that is. It's hard to compete with the mom."

"Yeah, that's true, I guess. So are you two progressing in the right direction?"

"We might be driving down the same street, but we definitely have two different destinations," I told her.

"Is he still keeping in contact with Cre'?"

"Well, he said no, so I'll just have to give him the benefit of the doubt. Anyway, not to be rude, but I really don't want to talk about him tonight. I want to be free of him this evening."

"Hold that thought, and do not turn around yet," Joi whispered.

"Why?"

"Because Tyree just walked in the club, with some chick on his arm."

"Oh no, he didn't."

"Oh yes, he did, and he doesn't look like he's stressed out, and there's no way that could be his mother unless she had him at the age of one."

My stomach started doing flip-flops. I felt like I couldn't breathe. I was so upset that it took every fiber in my body for me to keep it together. I could not let him know how upset I was.

"Joi, I'll be right back."

"Faith, don't go over there."

"I'm not."

I went to the ladies' room because I felt this overwhelming emotion. I wanted to go out there and slap him right in his damn face. I decided to channel my emotions with some poetry. I had some things that I needed to get off of my chest. I approached the club's manager, Dre.

"Dre? Can I go on tonight?" I asked.

"You know you always have a spot here. Anytime. As a matter of fact, you can go on right after this act," said Dre.

"Thanks."

"Are you all right?" he asked.

"Yeah, Dre. I will be."

I waited patiently while the act before me was finishing up. I looked into the crowd and saw Tyree with his date. I just shook my head. I looked around at our table, and Joi was sitting there like she didn't know what was about to go down. Finally, it was my turn.

Dre introduced me. "Ladies and gentlemen, our next poet is no stranger to the mic, and as usual, she puts her thing down. Let's give a warm welcome to my girl Faith."

Everybody began snapping their fingers.

I looked out at Tyree and noticed that his smile was gone, and he was looking a bit nervous.

I grabbed the mic. "Hi, everybody. Thanks for coming out. I would like to do another one of my personal creations, called . . . 'Shifty.'"

You're driving me crazy . . . shifting me to the left, right, back and forth . . . and now I'm back in the middle. . . .

In the middle of some bullshit that I'm not emotionally equipped to deal with.

I'm so confused because you say you need me and want me in your life, but this female is trippin' like she's your wife. . . .

One minute she's here; next minute she's gone . . .
  gone with the wind, but the wind must have
  changed its mind and blew her back again and
  again and again.
You say she's fatal . . . fatally attracted to you . . .
  trippin' out, tryin' to kill herself . . . just to hold
  on to her boo. . . .
We're not fatal, but she's killing us, too . . . the
  time we can't spend together, the love we don't
  make . . .
Baby, I love you . . . I just don't know how much
  more I can take. . . .
You're driving me crazy . . . shifting me to the left,
  right, back and forth . . . and now I'm back
  in the middle again. . . .
In the middle of some bullshit that I'm not emo-
  tionally equipped to deal with . . . I . . . quit!

The crowd gave me mad props. They started requesting some more, but that was all I had in me. As I was walking down off the stage, Joi and Tyree both met me at the same time. I caught Joi rolling her eyes and shaking her head at him.

"Yo, baby. This is not what you think," said Tyree.

But before I could respond, a young lady walked up behind him.

"Baby, I ordered us some drinks," she said. "Oh, by the way, your poem was slammin'. Honey, aren't you going to introduce us?"

"This is Faith," Tyree murmured.

"And your name?" I asked.

"Oh, babe, you forgot to tell her my name," the young woman said.

"I didn't get a chance to yet. I just came back here to get an autograph," Tyree lied.

"Oh, I'm his fiancée, Cre'ole. Cre' for short. Girl, like I said before, I truly enjoyed your poem. It sounds like you had someone in mind. Hmm, with all that drama, I would have kicked him to the curb," the young woman said, smiling and holding on to Tyree's arm.

I started to give her the same advice, because I was quite familiar with some of the bullshit he was putting her through, and she hadn't kicked his ass to the curb. I just had a feeling that she was checking up on Tyree and making sure we knew that she was his fiancée. I wasn't mad at her. She had to do what she had to do, and that was to claim her territory by any means necessary.

"Oh, trust me. I did," I said.

"Well, it was nice meeting you," said Cre'.

"It was nice meeting you, too," I replied.

"Faith, are you okay?" Joi asked.

"Yes. I'm fine. Now I have an idea of what you went through at Jaylen's wedding. Girl, how did you do it?"

"Yeah, it was rough."

"I'm not going to let Tyree spoil my evening. I'm just going to sit here and wait for Dave to come on and kick it with my best friend. I am so done with him. Cre', or Cre'ole, can have that headache."

Strike three!

Chapter 15

Cold Case

Joi

Man, I shouldn't have hung out last night. My body wasn't what it used to be. Work was killing me, and these criminal cases were piling up on my desk. I didn't have the energy to look at any of them.

I knew I had to figure out a game plan that would allow me the time to review at least five to ten files a day. I really did not have a choice, because I was due to report on each and every last one of them by this Friday.

"Shit. I need a cup of coffee," I mumbled.

As I got up from my desk, I knocked over two files. It pissed me off because I just did not have time to stoop down and sort through all this mess, but I knew that I had to make sure that the right paperwork was in the right place. I didn't have a choice. Nobody else was going to do it. I started sorting through some of the papers, and the headlines of a newspaper article caught my attention. RAPE VICTIM CLAIMS THAT SUSPECT HAS A STRANGE BIRTHMARK ON BUTTOCK. I read the article. Apparently, over on the east side of town, there were some unsolved rape cases. The suspect was described as an African American, stocky, six feet plus, early thirties, with a strange birthmark on his left buttock. I instantly dropped the folder. A weird feeling came over me, and I just froze for a minute.

Damon? I thought. *No freakin' way. Maybe it's a relative. It has to be, because Damon does not need to rape anybody. Shit, he may be a little crazy, but rape is a bit much.*

I went and got a cup of coffee in the break room and hurriedly walked back to my desk to review that particular file for any clues that would dispel any thoughts of Damon being a rapist. That five-to-ten file game plan just went out the window.

"Damon might have stalker capabilities, but a rapist? Nah!" I told myself.

Apparently, there had been another case linked to this one. The prosecution had indicated that they had some DNA evidence, but no primary suspect. I drank half of my coffee and continued reading through the file. I had managed to shut down everything else and had started focusing wholeheartedly on this case. The bottom line was that if Damon was somehow connected to any of these rapes, then I would be the biggest fool walking. The description was not as clear as I would have liked for it to be, which was probably a good thing. I still felt trapped. I just could not turn him in without feeling a sense of guilt, yet I had an obligation as an attorney and to the victims.

"Oh, Lord, I need you right about now. I need to pray on this one with everything inside of me. Just provide me the guidance to do the right thing," I prayed out loud.

Whew, I needed to call my boy Roc who free-lances as a private investigator to see if he had come up with any info on Damon.

I quickly dialed the number. "Hey, Roc. This is Joi."

"What's up?" said Roc.

"I don't know. You tell me."

"Well, my boy hasn't gotten back to me yet, but I will call him when we hang up, and I'll call you back."

"Look, Roc, I came across some information in one of my files, and I know this is a long shot, but I think Damon may be involved. You have to promise me that you will keep this information confidential."

"Not a problem. What's up?"

"Well, I received an anonymous tip. Someone gave me an envelope mentioning Damon's name, along with a newspaper article. Do you remember ever hearing about a rapist where the victim talked about a weird birthmark on the suspect's buttock?"

"Yeah, it was like a mouse or something. Right?"

"I'm not sure, Roc, because this is the first time I've read about it."

"So, Joi, why are you so freaked out about it?"

"Well, Roc, this is the part I need for you to keep to yourself for now."

"Okay. I'm listening," he said.

"Well, I don't know how to say this, so I'm just going to come straight out with it. Damon has a birthmark on his left buttock, and it is in the shape of Mickey Mouse."

"You've got to be shittin' me. Now that's some wild shit."

"I'm as serious as a heart attack. I need for you to check it out for me. I need to be sure. There are too many signs, and he is acting a little crazy. He keeps calling and hanging up, stalking me at the clubs, and now this."

"Do you mind if I see the file?" he asked.

"Yes, I do mind. I can be disbarred if I show you the file."

"Well, do you have anything we could use to get a DNA sample?" Roc asked.

"I'm not sure."

"Invite him over," he suggested.

"Have you lost your mind? The way things have been lately between us, I don't know what he might try."

"Do you have anything, like a present, card, or anything that he might have touched?"

"Let me think . . . Let me think . . . Let me think. Damn, this is too much, Roc," I moaned.

"Well, keep thinking. Did he ever touch any of your CDs?"

"Yes! Yes! He has touched just about all of them in my living room. I also have some cards with the envelopes that he sent to me. There may be some saliva on the stamps or something."

"Okay, calm down. Grab 'em up and meet me at the police station."

"Give me about an hour. I need to call my boss and give him an update. He won't present any of this information to your office unless he has concrete evidence."

"Okay. I'll see you in about an hour," Roc said.

My hands started trembling. I still had this horrible feeling inside of me. I wanted to do my job, but this was too much of a conflict of interest. If the rapist turned out to be Damon, I would be devastated. I could see the headlines now. ATTORNEY WAS A STREET-SMART DUMMY.

I really needed to call Jaylen, because he would know just what to do to calm me down, but I knew that I couldn't just pick up the phone and call him. His wife would trip out. For a minute, my heart just sank thinking about him. I thought my missing him would have eased up by now, but it had only become magnified. It was like I had put my feelings for him on layaway somewhere in my heart, and every now and then, I got this reminder that he was still there, waiting for me to come for him.

"Oh, Jaylen, I'm missing you so much right now. Why did you give up on us? I have so much going on in my life right now. I already lost you, and now I might be losing Lex. If only I could talk to you," I said aloud, crying.

I got myself together and called my boss to explain everything to him. He said that he was on his way down to the station to meet me. I drove to my house to pick up the potential evidence. I grabbed about twenty CDs, cards, and letters, along with a pair of gloves, and placed them in a tote bag and immediately left, heading toward the police station.

Ring . . . ring . . .

"Hello?"

"Hel-lo, Joi," a male voice said.

"Who is this?" I asked.

"Damon."

For a quick moment, my heart just froze. Why was he calling me now? Was he following me? Did he know what I was up to? I finally managed to muster up enough guts to respond.

"Oh, hi."

"Look, I know that I'm the last person that you want calling you, but I've been acting like a fool lately, and I wanted to apologize. I mean, you, of all people, do not deserve to be treated like that. It was just difficult for me to understand that you did not want me, and that's cool, but it still should not have ever happened."

"Thanks for the apology, Damon," I said nonchalantly.

"So, does that mean you will accept my apology? I mean, if you're not ready to accept my apology, then I understand. Maybe one day we can be friends again."

"I'll think about it. I have another call. I'll keep in touch, Damon."

"All right. I'm out. Peace."

Click.

"Hello," I said, sounding frustrated.

"Where are you at, Joi?" Roc asked.

"I'm about a block away from the station. I should be there in less than a minute," I replied.

"Meet me at my car before you go in. I have some more information for you about your boy, Damon."

"Oh, okay. By the way, he just called me. I'll fill you in with all the details when I see you."

As I approached the police station, it looked somewhat deserted. There were only about three police cars in the parking lot. As I drove around the building, I saw Roc's little blue, beat-up Volkswagen parked on the side. I swore he needed a bigger car. He was just entirely too big for that car. He looked like biscuits trying to escape out of a busted can. He knew that I couldn't fit inside that car with him, so he was going to need to come and get inside my ride.

Toot, toot went my horn.

"Roc? What's up? Come and get inside my truck," I yelled.

"Give me a minute," he said.

Finally, he slowly got out of his vehicle and got into mine.

"So, what else did you find out?" I asked nervously.

"Well, my boy called me back. He found out that your boy, Damon, has a secret past from his sophomore year in college."

"What kind of past?" I asked.

"He was charged with statutory rape when he was nineteen years old. He had sex with over a dozen underage girls. Only one came forward and pressed charges. She claimed that he forced himself on her. He claimed that they were dating and that the sex was consensual. The charges were later dropped because they did not have enough evidence. However, some felt that because he was a big football star with a promising career, something was done to make it go away," Roc explained.

Ring . . . ring.

"Hold that thought. It's my mom." I answered the call. "Hello, Mom. Can I call you back?"

"Joi, I know you are busy, but Alexis is not doing that well," said Mom.

"So, what are you saying exactly?" I said in a confused state.

"I'm just saying that you need to get here as soon as possible," said Mom.

"Oh, okay. I will be there as soon as I leave the police station," I replied.

"Police station? Is everything okay?" she asked.

"Yeah, it's just work related," I assured her.

"Well, I'll see you when you get there. Some of the family already went up to the hospital."

Sniffing, I replied, "I have to go, Mom. I love you."

"Everything okay, Joi?" Roc asked.

"Not really. My aunt Alexis is not doing so well, and I need to go to the hospital."

"Go handle your business with your family, and I will take it from here."

"But—"

"Look, Joi, you're my girl, and your family needs you. I got this. Go handle your business," he insisted.

"You're right. Thank you, Roc. You always look out for me."

Roc gave me a hug and sent me on my way. I knew he would handle the situation. He treated me like I was his little sister. I could trust him with just about anything.

Chapter 16

Letting Go!

Joi

Three weeks later . . .

I was a nervous wreck. I kept thinking that this might be it for Lex. What was the real story with Damon? Life was a bitch. I needed to calm down and get myself together. Everybody expected me to be the strong one. I was not allowed to crumble, because I was a superwoman. Well, about right now, I was ready to give up my cape. I had to handle these two situations separately before I got confused and crazy. My main priority right now was Lex.

Why is the family up there again? I thought as I drove to the hospital.

I just hoped and prayed that she was still alive.

There was nothing worse than going up to the hospital and finding that the person was already dead. I remembered when my godfather died from a major heart attack. The entire room had frozen when I'd entered. I hadn't known what to do. They'd made me feel like it was my turn to trip. I'd just walked over to him and kissed his forehead and cried next to his side. I had not wanted anyone to console me in that room. Boy, I needed to talk to Jaylen.

"Jaylen, I really need you now. I wish you were here," I cried out loud.

I took out my cell phone and dialed his number. *Ring . . . ring.*

His machine answered. I waited for his message to finish so that I could leave one after the beep.

"Jay, this is Joi. Call me when you get a chance. It's important," I said, my voice cracking.

I continued to slowly drive to the hospital. I just could not bear any bad news. I could not imagine losing Aunt Alexis. She was my best friend. I finally arrived at the hospital and parked my car in the emergency-room parking lot. I walked in and immediately bumped into my mom.

"How is she?" I asked.

"Not good. Craig is talking to the doctors right now."

"About what?"

"Well, the cancer has spread all through her body, and they want to know whether or not to keep her alive on a machine, if it becomes necessary," Mom said.

"Where is she now?"

"They put her in room three."

I walked into her room, and she was sitting up next to the nurse, rocking back and forth.

"Joi, I'm tired," Lex whispered.

"I know, Lex. Just lie down," I told her.

"No, Joi. I'm tired of being sick. I'm ready to go now."

I was crying so badly on the inside, I could not respond, because I had a huge knot in my throat. Finally, I said, "It's okay. Just lie down."

"I don't want any machines keeping me alive."

"Okay, Aunt Lex," I whispered.

I held her tightly and rubbed her back until my aunt Mary, Craig, and my mom returned. It was obvious that they were upset, but they did not want to show it in front of Aunt Alexis.

I left and drove to my parents' house. I did not want to be at my place alone with everything going on with Damon and Lex.

"Are you okay, Daughter?" my dad asked.

"Not really," I replied.

"She's going to be all right. Just keep praying for her. She is strong," he said.

I checked my cell, and to my surprise, Jaylen had left me three messages.

"Joi, this is Jaylen. Please call me." *Beep*.

"Joi, this is Jay. You didn't sound too good. Call me as soon as you get this message." *Beep*.

"Joi, call me. It does not matter what time."

Mmm, let me call him before I fall asleep. If any-body can make me feel better, it is Jaylen.

Ring . . . ring.

"Hello?"

"Hey, Jay."

"Joi, girl, what's going on? You sound like you lost your best friend."

"It's my aunt Lexie."

"What's wrong with Lex?"

I filled him in on what had gone on with Lex since we last spoke. I didn't want to talk about Damon. I could handle only one thing at a time.

"I'm on my way over," he said.

"No, I'm not home. I'm at my parents' house."

"Do you want me to come there?" he asked.

"No, I know you're home with your wife, but thanks, anyway."

Suddenly there was silence on Jaylen's end of the phone.

"Anyway, I'm tired," I added. "I'm going to try to get some sleep because I need to be up at the hospital first thing in the a.m."

"Call me and let me know how she is doing."

"I sure will, Jay. Thanks for being there."

"There's no other place I'd rather be," he said softly.

I did not know how to take his comment, so I just left it alone for now and hung up. I finally dozed off.

"Joi, Joi, wake up," Mom said, shaking me.

"What's wrong?"

My heart was beating fast. It was five in the morning. I heard my sister crying and screaming downstairs, but I could not make sense of it.

"Lex passed," Mom said.

"Lex passed what?" I said.

"She died about a half an hour ago. The hospital called and told Craig, Aunt Mary, and Uncle James."

"No! Mom, please don't say that," I said.

I jumped up, threw on my same clothes, and sped to the hospital. When I arrived, it was like the staff at the hospital knew who I was and just let me walk through with no pass. As I made my way to her room, I heard the family screaming and crying. I walked into the room, and Craig was holding Lex in his arms.

"Lex, wake up, baby. Wake up. Please don't leave me. I'm sorry. I love you. Please, wake up," he cried.

"Craig, she's gone," Aunt Mary and Uncle James said.

"No, she's not. She's still breathing. Come on, babe. Wake up. Please, wake up," Craig said, crying.

I just looked at Lex lying there on the bed, with her mouth slightly open, as if she were sleeping peacefully. For some odd reason, at that very moment, I felt relieved that she was not suffering anymore. I was sad yet relieved.

Craig's mother and the rest of the family were finally able to convince Craig that Lex was gone. My cousin Amelia was so sad. It was like she had lost her sister. I just gave her a big hug.

"She's not suffering anymore, Amelia," I soothed.

"I know. I'm just going to miss her so much," she said.

"We all are," I said.

I felt like the walls were caving in on me; I had to leave. Just as I turned around to make my exit, I bumped into Jaylen.

"Jaylen! What are you doing here?" I said.

"I called your parents' house this morning to check on you, and your father told me what had happened. I had to come," he replied.

Out of nowhere, I just kneeled down on the floor and put my head in my hands and cried. I just could not believe Lex was gone. I was mad because I should have been there when she died. I could have spent the night. Jaylen knelt down next to me and lifted me up. He was the only one I could let my guard down with. He knew the weak side of me. I did not have to be a superwoman in front of him. It felt good knowing I could let go when I needed to.

Jaylen drove me home and stayed with me for hours. I wanted to ask him about Toni, but I didn't want to spoil the moment.

"Jaylen, thanks for coming. You're always there for me," I told him.

"I wouldn't want to be anywhere else."

Chapter 17

The Finale

Joi

Knock, knock, knock!

"Just a minute. I'm coming," I called.

I walked toward the door half asleep. I was in another world, but the sound of the loud knocking had shocked me out of my sleep.

"Ouch! Shit, I hit my knee," I yelled.

I started limping to the door. Now I was completely awake.

"Who is it?" I called.

"It's Eboni, Taj, and Faith," they said in unison.

I opened the door, and they rushed in like it was an emergency.

"Joi, we heard about Lex. Is there anything we can do?" Faith asked.

"No, I'm fine. She's in a better place now," I replied.

"She's with the angels now," Taj said.

"I didn't know she was that sick, Joi," Faith said.

Eboni wasn't saying much of anything. She seemed like she was in shock. Her emotions seemed to be crippled.

"Eb, are you all right?" I asked.

"Yeah, girl. I'm just trying to grasp all of this," she said while holding my hand.

I had never seen Eboni like this before. She seemed like she was smiling to keep from crying.

They stayed with me all day. We sat around and watched television. They answered most of my calls from family and friends. I did speak to my immediate family. I just couldn't handle talking about Lex and what had happened. It was too much. The telephone rang again around 4:15 p.m. It was Jaylen.

"Hi, Jaylen. This is Taj. Yes, she is here, but she is resting right now."

"Oh no, Taj. I'll take Jay's call," I said anxiously.

"Oh, hold on, Jay. She'll take your call," Taj said, giving me a look that said "Excuse the hell outta me."

"Hello, Jaylen," I whispered.

"How are you doing, Joi?"

"I'm hanging in there, I guess," I said.

"I wanted to stop by later on to check on you and talk to you about something. That is, if it is okay with you."

"What do you want to talk about?" I said.

"I'd rather discuss it in person."

"What time?"

"Around seven tonight."

"Cool."

I hung up the telephone, and now Taj had this crazy look on her face. "What was that all about?" she quizzed.

"Jay wants to talk to me about something. He wouldn't tell me over the phone. He said that he would stop by later on," I explained.

"Well, I'm not going anywhere. I'm staying if he's coming," Taj proclaimed.

"That won't be necessary, Taj. I'll be fine," I insisted.

"What does a married man want with his ex? Sex?" Taj asked.

"No, it's not like that," I explained. "Jay came to the hospital yesterday and stayed with me for a couple of hours. It was completely innocent. However, he was acting like something was wrong."

"What was he doing there?" Taj asked.

"I called him," I replied.

"Why?" Faith asked.

I wanted to just tell them how Jaylen and I really felt about each other. I needed Jaylen, and he needed me, too. My aunt Alexis was gone now, and it made me realize that tomorrow wasn't promised. Jaylen loved me and I loved him, and if we could make this work, so be it. I decided not to go there with Taj, Faith, and Eboni.

"I asked you a question," Faith reminded me after a few seconds of silence.

"Well, Faith, with everything going on with Damon and Lex, I had to talk to someone," I explained.

"Damon?" Eboni asked.

"What about Damon?" Faith asked in a demanding voice.

"I really cannot go there right now. Just know that it is serious, and I will tell you guys when I find out more," I assured them.

"Well, just as long as you know that we're here for you," Faith remarked.

"Thanks," I said.

"We won't talk about it right now with everything going on with Lex," said Eboni.

"Well, I have to meet up with my family to discuss the funeral arrangements, so I'll catch up with you guys later," I said.

"Are you sure you're not rushing us out because of Jaylen?" asked Taj.

"Nah, he won't be here until later on," I replied.

"Just remember that he is married," Faith cautioned.

"No kidding. Trust me. I know," I assured them.

After they left, I got dressed and headed over to my aunt Mary and uncle James's house. It was somewhat crowded, but organized. Everyone seemed to have some sort of an assignment to handle. They asked my cousin Amelia and me to write a poem. They wanted us to read it at the funeral. I told them that I would have to think about it, because I might be a wreck on that day. The family seemed sad, yet they were coping. The kids, including Lex's son, Brandon, were outside playing in the backyard. I stared at Brandon and called him over to see how he was doing.

"Brandon?" I said.

"Yes," he murmured.

"Are you okay?"

"Yes."

"I'm going to come and pick you up next week and take you to Great Adventure. Would you like to go?"

"Yeah! Can I bring one of my friends?" he asked.

"Sure. Let me know who, and I will call his mom and dad to make sure he can go with us. Give me a hug, boy. I love you, and if you ever need anything, just call me."

"Okay," he said, with a sad smile.

The funeral was scheduled for Saturday morning. There would be a private viewing for the family on Friday evening. Relatives I hadn't seen in years started showing up, with food and drinks. I had forgotten how big our family was. Craig was nowhere to be found. I did not really want to see his face right now, anyway. I started searching for my mom to see if she needed me for anything before I left.

"Mom, I'm about to leave. Do you need me for anything before I go?"

"No, baby, go home and get some rest. You look tired." She looked me over and gave me a big hug and kissed me on my cheek.

"Love you, Mom."

"I love you, too, Joi Nicole."

I made my way to my car. Just before I started up the engine, my cell phone rang.

"Hello?" I said.

"Joi, this is Roc. I know you got a lot going on, but I wanted you to know that we got him."

"Got who?" I asked.

"Damon."

"Oh my gosh! For real? How? When? Sorry, Roc. I'm trippin' with everything that is going on."

"Where are you at, Joi?"

"I'm just leaving my relatives' house up on the hill," I told him.

"Can you meet me at the Hamburger Palace on Fifth and Main Street in ten minutes?"

"Sure," I responded.

I started driving really fast because I was so anxious to know what was going on with Damon. But then I took a deep breath to calm myself down before I ended up having an accident. I was one light away from the Hamburger Palace. I could see Roc's little hoopdie parked on the side. I drove up next to him and hopped out of the car. He rolled down his window.

"So what happened?" I asked anxiously.

"His fingerprints on your CDs matched the fingerprints from the evidence lab. The detectives are still checking out the DNA evidence."

"What did Damon say?"

"He said he was innocent and these allegations were ridiculous. He also contacted his attorney."

"Does he know it was me who turned him in?" I asked.

"Not to my knowledge," replied Roc.

"Well, how did you convince him to go down to the station?"

"The po-po went to his house and asked him if he could come down to the station to answer some questions about a rape in the area a little over a year ago."

"I'm surprised he didn't snap out, because he does have a temper."

"They stroked his ego by acknowledging his pro football highlights and reassured him that this was most likely a big misunderstanding, and he agreed."

"Whoa!" I exclaimed.

Roc went on. "They also wanted to get another set of his prints on their own, to be absolutely sure. However, in the meantime, he is at the police station, being processed. After that they are on lockdown at the Somberta County jail."

"Thanks for the update and especially for taking over and handling this situation for me. I really don't want him to know I turned him in, because he may try to come after me."

Roc gave me that you-know-I'll-do-anything-for-you-without-asking look. I squeezed his hand and mouthed a silent thank-you. I could feel his eyes staring at me as I walked back to my car. Opening my car door, I waved a good-bye and drove off. I just hoped he wasn't starting to like me, because I was not feeling him like that. He was like family to me.

I headed up the highway, toward my house. Jaylen would be there in about forty-five minutes, and I needed to regroup and get myself together.

I opened my front door and went inside, picking up my mail on the way. I went through my bills, tossing the junk mail in the trash. Then I poured myself a glass of red wine to calm my nerves. I didn't know why, but I had mixed emotions about setting Damon up. Trust me, if he did commit those crimes, he deserved everything he had coming to him. I just didn't want to get caught up in the drama. I wanted to spare myself the embarrassment. I sat down and started listening to my stereo system. I put on the smooth jazz CD that I had purchased at Target last week.

Knock, knock, knock.

"Coming!" I yelled.

As I walked to the door, I could hear Jaylen on his cell. I opened the door, with my hands on my hips.

"Hello, Jay."

"Hello to you, too," he said, smiling.

He then whipped out a bouquet of flowers.

"Thanks. They're beautiful. What's the occasion?"

"No special reason. Just because."

I put the flowers in a vase with some water. We then walked into the family room. I wanted to know once and for all what was going on in his life.

"So, Jay, what's up?"

"Joi, I know you've been wondering why I am always by myself. You know, without Toni," he said.

"That's true, so why?"

"Well, shortly after she got pregnant, I noticed how close she had become to her ex-husband. He became more significant than me."

"What do you mean, close? Did he come over to the house?" I quizzed.

"No, not to my knowledge, anyway. I mean, they talked just about every day on the telephone. She didn't even try to hide it."

"Did you ever question their relationship?"

"Hell yeah. She said that they were just really good friends, like you and I. I really couldn't say much, because she did have a point."

"And what point is that, Jaylen?" I asked.

"The point is that she had finally started respecting our relationship, so I needed to respect hers. It is what it is," he explained.

"That's just an excuse to get at you because of me."

"Well, at the end of the day, I could care less. My main concern is that baby she is carrying in her stomach."

"I hear what you're saying, Jay."

"I took your advice and tried to work on my marriage. That's why you have not heard from me recently. I was just trying to stay focused and give it one hundred percent."

Jay told me that he had continued to notice some strange things about Toni. She just did not seem to be in tune with the whole marriage thing. He initially thought it had something to do with the pregnancy, but it was more than that. They tried to work on it. They talked to a marriage counselor, their pastor, and family members, but they just did not seem to connect. He soon realized that their marriage was a mistake. After that, everything else just went downhill. She gave nothing to the marriage.

"Oh, she definitely has it twisted. But you still need to find out what the deal is with her ex-husband. By the way, who in the hell is he? What's the ex-husband's name?"

"Kenyatta Jones," he said.

"Why does his name sound so familiar, Jay? Kenyatta, Kenyatta. Let me think. Ooh, I can't put my finger on it, but it will come to me."

"Well, you know me. I'm one step ahead of you. I handled my business and asked him man-to-man what was up with him and Toni," said Jaylen.

"So, what did he say?"

"First, he tried to convince me that they were just good friends. So I invited him to stop by one day so that I could meet him."

"Then what? Did he come by?" I asked.

"Yeah, he came."

"Uh, come on, Jay. What happened next? You're making me pull it out of you. What happened after that?"

"I recognized him from the cruise," he said matter-of-factly.

"Stop the madness, Jay. Is Kenyatta K. J.?"

"Yup. The wife this dude was talking about the whole time was actually *my* wife. He told me that he had never stopped loving Toni and that our marriage was a big mistake and that there was so much I didn't know."

"Wait, Jaylen. I need a minute to digest this information. First of all, what in the hell was he doing on the same ship?" I said.

"He said Toni made the reservations, and she purchased an additional cabin for him. She had planned on spending time with both of us."

"Well, they should have never divorced each other if they can't be away from each other."

"I know. I was just so shocked about what he told me that I didn't want to even begin trying to understand Toni's motives. He went on to tell me that when he'd invited Toni and me to dinner, he had planned on telling me everything, but she'd begged him not to. Obviously, they were meeting up on the ship, which would explain all of Toni's disappearing acts. She'd even had the nerve to tell him that she just needed more time because I had recently come into some money, and she felt that she was entitled to at least half. Then he dropped the bomb."

"What bomb?"

"He said that there was a strong possibility that the baby might not be mine, but his."

"Get the hell out of here. This sounds like some R. Kelly crap. Sorry, Jay. You blew me away with that one. I was not prepared for this. Whew."

He shook his head. "Yeah, well, imagine how I felt. I was crushed. I mean, I was really getting excited about being a father. Now I find out that this innocent baby might not be mine. That is some straight-up bullshit."

"Did you two get into a fight?" I asked.

"For what? My marriage was already on the rocks, so he just helped me to understand some things. As crazy as it may sound, I'm glad he told me."

"Oh, Jaylen, I'm sorry you have to go through this. Toni is a hot mess."

"I'm cool. I just have to man up and get a paternity test. I need to know."

"Did she agree?" I asked.

"She has no choice. With or without her, I'm going to get the test done. But she tried to convince me that the baby is mine. She never cheated on me, according to her."

"So, do you think the baby is yours?" I asked him point-blank.

"Let me put it to you this way. I keep having reoccurring thoughts of being on *Maury*, Maury Povich's show, and having them say, 'You are *not* the father!'"

"Well, maybe you should call *Maury*. I would love to see her ass run off the stage, crying."

"No, she'll get hers," Jaylen said.

"Mmm . . . I just knew Ms. Toni was a phony. It was just something about her that I could not put my finger on at the time. So, I take it that you do believe the ex-husband might be the father?"

"Yup," he said, shaking his head in slow motion.

"So, where are you at with everything, with your marriage and stuff?" I probed.

"Well, I packed up all my stuff and just left a month ago. It hurts because I really want a son or daughter. The baby is due in a few months, and if it turns out that I am the father, I will be there for my child. However, I needed to move on now because I came across some incriminating information that proves she was never divorced from her alleged ex-husband, Kenyatta Jones."

"So, are you getting a divorce?"

"I had the marriage annulled based on fraud," he murmured.

"So she is a bigamist?"

"Yes, she is."

"Is there anything I can do for you, Jay?"

"I'm fine, Joi. I'm here to take care of you right now."

"Where are you staying?" I asked.

"With my brother, Jordan," he replied. "So, stop trying to avoid the subject. What is going on with you and Damon? I heard a whole lot of crazy shit, and I want you to tell me about it."

"Who told you?" I asked.

"It's not about who told me. You should have told me."

"I think we've heard enough crazy stuff for one day," I replied.

"Hey, Joi, you listened to me. Now I want to listen to you. Let's clear the air."

I filled him in on everything pertaining to Damon. I told him about the e-mails, the hang-up calls, stalking me at the clubs. I even told him that Damon was a suspect in a rape case. He couldn't believe it. Jaylen knew of Damon from when he played in the NFL. Damon just did not fit the prototype that I was describing. I had to show Jaylen some of the e-mails, and I also had him listen to the messages Damon had left me.

Jaylen shook his head. "Well, thank goodness, he is locked up. Because if he tries to hurt you, Joi, I will hurt him."

"Let's not talk about Damon anymore tonight. He is locked up at the Somberta County jail, and hopefully, he will get the rehabilitation he needs. But enough about him. I have some other things I need to take care of personally."

"Do you need my help?"

"No, I got it. I need to cancel my trip to Jamaica this week. With the funeral being this Saturday, I just cannot go."

I made my way to the kitchen to get us something to drink. I was so glad we were talking. I felt a lot better and, hopefully, I would get a good night's sleep. After I poured myself something to drink, I silently screamed, *yes!*

I wasn't happy about his family breaking up. I was just happy because I felt like I had just been given a second chance with Jaylen. We had found each other again. There I went again, jumping to conclusions. He might not even want me anymore. We both just had so much baggage.

Jaylen stayed for a couple of hours, and then he went home. I stayed in bed for most of the next two days, leaving only to attend Lex's private viewing. At the private viewing, I was overwhelmed and also sad. I was basically depressed. Afterward, my cousin Amelia called to see if I had any input on the poem. I told her that I would give her my portion this morning, before the funeral. I did not have anything prepared, but I knew what Lex meant to me, and right about now, I was not going to be concerned if my words rhymed or not. I'd jot down something.

My telephone rang constantly. I would just look at the caller ID. Every time I dozed off, the telephone would ring. I finally decided to get myself together. I didn't want to go to this funeral. I was just not there mentally. Last night, the private viewing had been too much for the family. Everyone had been crying and stuff. I'd tried to be strong, especially for her son, but everyone was making some of the others' efforts useless. I hated feeling like this. I was glad I had some extra time off, which was really my vacation time.

I put on a black dress, some basic black shoes, and some shades. Then I drove to the church so that I could meet up with Amelia and give her my portion of the poem. The church parking lot was packed. There were cars everywhere. I saw my mom and sister a few steps ahead of me.

"Hi, Mom," I called.

"Hey, Joi. How are you holding up?" Mom asked.

"I'm okay as long as I'm out here. What about you?"

"We already went inside. It's just so hot in there," Mom said.

"Well, the family is starting to line up. We had better go," I said.

I walked in with my dad, mom, and sister. We lined up next to each other, along with other relatives. Everyone walked up to view the body again. Some cried and some fell out. Most of us kissed Lex's forehead and kneeled to say a prayer. After we finally sat down, the funeral started. The service was beautiful. Tina sang "Don't Cry for Me," by CeCe Winans. The pastor preached until he couldn't preach anymore. He had the family up on their feet, telling us to celebrate Lex's life because to be absent from the body was to be present with the Lord. "Hallelujah," he said.

"Amen," someone shouted.

The pastor's wife read a select few of the beautiful cards and poems dedicated to Lex, and then people got up and spoke so highly of her. My girls lined up and said some really nice things also. However, when Eboni got up, she talked about Lex and how much she meant to all of us, but she also talked about her sister Tori, and how she'd lost her battle to cancer as a teenager.

I did not know Eboni had a sister that died of cancer, I thought. All this time, she had never mentioned it to me. I asked Taj and Faith about Eboni's sister, and they didn't know anything, either. Maybe it was devastating for Eboni, and she had buried it away until now. That would probably explain why she was acting odd when she, Taj, and Faith came to my house after Lex passed. She'd been so quiet and withdrawn.

After Eboni spoke, the pastor said some final words. Tina ended everything by singing another gospel song. She had such a beautiful voice.

Finally, the service was over. The repast was at my aunt and uncle's home. I stayed for about an hour, but I had to leave. This whole day had been a drain. Jaylen had attended the funeral with his brother, Jordan. He asked me if I was on my way home, so I told him yes. He asked if he could stop by, and I told him yes again.

As soon as I pulled up in front of my house, Jaylen was there. He helped me carry some food and bags inside. After we put everything away in the refrigerator, he went and sat down on the couch. I sat down next to him. He pulled me close to him.

"Joi, I need to ask you something."

"What, Jay?"

"Look, I know we're both feeling vulnerable right now because of the situations going on in our lives, but I want you to know that this has nothing to do with how I feel about you."

"What are you saying exactly?"

"I'm saying that you, Joi, represent the joy that is missing in my life. You are and have always been my confidante and my best friend. I'm back now, and I want to love, honor, and protect you. I want you to feel safe again. We both made our mistakes, and believe me, I learned from them."

"Whew, Jay. So much time has passed. I just don't want to be your rebound, and I don't want you to stick around just because of my situation with Damon."

"I can't force my feelings on you, but they are real, and I'm not going anywhere. I married a woman that I didn't really know. I chose her for her outer beauty and physical attributes that resemble yours. But beauty is only skin-deep, and I had to learn the hard way. You are the total package. You are beautiful inside and out. You have everything I could ever need and want. She was my rebound for you."

"Well, maybe you need more time to clear your head," I said.

"My head is very clear. It is clear enough to ask you to marry me."

"Marry you? Jay, I'm sorry, but I cannot talk about this right now."

"Joi, this is the second time I've asked you. Just think about it. Don't give up on us."

"I know, Jay. I'm not giving up on us, but I need some more time to think about things."

"Things like what?" he quizzed.

"Everything, Jay. We both have been through hell and back. You don't know if this baby your ex-wife is carrying is yours or not. If for some reason it is, what arrangements are you going to make to ensure a stable environment for your child and me? You know Toni hates me, and she'll make your life a living hell."

"I'll cross that bridge when I come to it. I don't even know if the baby is mine," he said.

"Yeah, Jay, that is true, but look at my situation. I was dating a rapist who started stalking me. What does that say about my judgment when it comes to men? I'm supposed to be smarter than that. I know better, and I need to sort it out."

Chapter 18

Crossroads

Joi

Jaylen and I had been spending a lot of time together. He was dead set on us getting married. I was just a little apprehensive because neither of us had had a successful relationship with our previous partners. Jaylen and Toni's relationship had been all jacked up, and I'd been dating a rapist. Our story sounded like a cross between *Forensic Files* and *The Jerry Springer Show*. I loved Jaylen, but I was scared. I felt like our relationship was at a crossroads, and I didn't know which way to turn. I needed to call Jaylen right away.

"Jay, it's Joi."

"Hey, everything all right?"

"I wish. I just have so much I need to say to

you, but I don't know how. I always thought that I could talk to you about anything, and now I feel different."

"Different how, Joi?"

"Hesitant and unsure."

"About us?"

"Yes," I told him.

"Well, I see where you are coming from, and I'm willing to do anything to get us back to where we used to be."

"So, are you willing to go to a counselor with me?"

"Girl, I'd walk to the moon with you if I thought it would help," he replied.

"You are so crazy. Thanks for making me smile. Well, I found this psychologist in the area that we can go and talk to. Just let me know what your schedule is so that I can make the appointment."

"Just make the appointment, and I'll make the time to be there."

"All righty then. I'll call you in about an hour. I have something I need to handle."

"Okay. Call me later. I love you."

"I love you, too, Jay."

Wow, that was easy. I had thought Jay was going to be pissed, but he wasn't. I just hoped this psychologist was as good as everyone said she was. I wanted us to acknowledge our mistakes to avoid any future ones. I wanted us to further explore the different areas of counseling, such as financial counseling and spiritual counseling.

There were so many couples who got married, only to get divorced because they had failed to handle their finances properly. I wanted us to save our money and make sensible decisions together. It would be nice to have a diversified stock portfolio, life insurance, and mortgage insurance in the event that one of us got sick or had an untimely demise. I wanted us to raise a family and bond spiritually. Our children would hopefully become who we were now, not who we were back then. I just wanted somebody who was on point with me. Jay meant the world to me, but we needed to do this right. I planned on getting married only once, and divorce would not be an option for me.

I dialed the psychologist's number. "Hello. May I speak to Dr. Coleman?" I said.

"This is Dr. Coleman. How may I help you?"

"Oh, Dr. Coleman. This is Joi Thompson."

"Oh, hi, Joi. How may I help you?"

"Well, last time I spoke to you on the telephone, I told you that my fiancé and I were thinking about getting married, but we needed some counseling."

"When are you available?" Dr. Coleman asked.

"Anytime."

"How's tomorrow, around one thirty?"

"We'll be there."

"Okay. See you then."

Yes, we were making progress. The first step was admitting that you had a problem. I called Jay back and gave him the appointment information.

"Hello, Jaylen. This is Joi."

"Hey, baby. What's up?"

"I spoke to Dr. Coleman, and our appointment is tomorrow at one thirty. So meet me here at my house at one o'clock, and we can go together."

"You're not playin'?"

"No, I'm not, and neither should you," I growled.

"Calm down, Joi. It was a joke."

"I know, Jaylen. I just want to move on beyond this point. I feel inadequate, and I hate feeling this way."

"I understand. I'll be prompt."

Jaylen was busy expanding his investment firm with some of the money he'd received from Mrs. Felton. He had so much going on and so little time to get it done. He was always in meetings with investors, attorneys, and business colleagues. He was so tired from work, we barely had time for each other. I tried to go to his place and cook him a good meal at least three times a week.

Jaylen wanted us to get close again on an intimate level, but I wanted us to be celibate during this period of transition for us. As much as I would have liked to, I knew that it would confuse things for us. Besides, he knew that we both needed to get tested. I didn't play with that. I had always made sure that Damon wore condoms, but his wife had been sleeping around on him with K. J., or whatever his name was, so there was no telling where any of them had been.

I needed to call my girl Faith to see what

she had been up to. She was getting ready to graduate from RN school. I was so proud of her. I needed to call Taj and Eboni so we could plan something nice for her. But first, I needed to call Faith.

"Hey, Faith. It's Joi."

"Hey, girl. I was just thinking about you. I'm so sorry I wasn't able to call you back last night. I've been busy prepping for my graduation next week."

"That's what's up, girl. You always did want to be a nurse, ever since you were in the second grade."

"How did you remember that? It was so long ago."

"Because I was the patient ninety-nine percent of the time. You were always taking sticks and poking me in my arm, like they were needles," I reminded her.

"Oh my gosh, you don't forget nothing," she teased.

"I know."

"Well, what about you? Every time we did something wrong, you would lock us up in jail, and we couldn't come out and play until we said the magic word."

"And what was the magic word?" I asked.

"The hell if I knew. You just made up words as they came. It was all good and obviously worth it. At least we knew what we wanted to be when we grew up."

"Faith, you're crazy," I said and laughed.

"I know, but it takes one crazy person to know a crazy person."

"So, how's the job search?" I asked.

"I forgot to tell you that I got offered a new job at the hospital, in the psychiatric department."

"See, I just told you that you was crazy."

"Whatever. They're paying me thirty-eight dollars an hour."

"Wow, that's great."

"I know, and I can work overtime if I want to," she added.

"So what exactly will you be doing?"

"From what they told me, I'll be working with the long-term patients. I will evaluate them and determine their courses of treatment. I have to go through a training program for a couple of weeks."

"Well, you deserve it," I told her. "I saw how hard you worked to become a registered nurse, and here you are."

"Thank you so much for being there for me. You're not only my best friend. You're like my sister, and I love you, Joi."

"Would you stop it? I don't feel like crying on this telephone. So on a lighter note, we want to take you out to celebrate."

"Well, can we wait until next week?" she asked.

"Sure. I'll let Taj and Eboni know," I told her and ended the call.

I was sitting here, trying to be a superwoman for everybody else. Shoot. I had a job to do. Some changes had been made in my office. My old boss had been transferred, and we were operating with a full staff again. Although I didn't have the additional workload anymore, I was still extremely busy. I had to take half a day tomorrow so that Jaylen and I could go and talk to Dr. Coleman.

I had so much that I wanted to tell her, but I didn't know how she was going to structure the session. It was costing us eighty-five dollars an hour, but we needed to go. Throughout the day, I kept asking myself what I was going say first, second, and third. Dr. Coleman might even have Jaylen go first. Who knew?

Finally, it was five o'clock, and I was done working for the day. I went to the grocery store to pick up a few items so that I could cook dinner for Jay. He loved Italian, so I figured I would make spaghetti and meatballs with angel-hair pasta. I picked up the pasta, hamburger meat, and spaghetti sauce. I almost forgot to pick up the garlic toast. I couldn't eat my spaghetti without it. I paid for the food and left the store. I drove over to Jaylen's so that I could cook dinner before he arrived.

I boiled the water for the pasta, and I started making the meat sauce. I figured that I would put the garlic toast in the oven after the main course was done. After I drained the pasta, I set the table and added candles and a bottle of wine that I found in his cabinet.

I wanted us to have a relaxing evening for a change. I knew that there were a lot of good shows coming on tonight, so I figured we might as well snuggle up and watch television. The pasta was finally done, so I put the garlic toast in the oven. I called Jaylen to see where he was.

"Hello."

"Jaylen?"

"Yes, dear?"

"Are you close to home?" I asked.

"Yes, I am. I'm right around the corner. Is everything okay?"

"No."

"What's the matter?" he asked.

"I'm just missing you, so hurry up."

Within five minutes, Jaylen came through the door. He looked at the table setting, along with the food, wine, and candles. "What did I do to deserve you? You didn't have to go out of your way and cook."

"Well, I wanted to. You've been swamped at the office, and you deserve a relaxing evening." I paused. "Are you ready for our appointment with Dr. Coleman tomorrow?"

"As ready as I'm ever going to be," he replied.

"Don't forget, it's at one thirty."

"I know, sweetheart."

"I almost forgot, Jaylen. I need you to meet me there instead of at the house. Is that okay? I'll leave the directions on the table."

"Okay, baby," he said, with a smile.

We ate dinner and drank some wine. Jaylen refused to let me clean up the kitchen. He made me sit down and relax. I was going to go home, but I decided to stay. I lay in his arms, watching television, until we both fell asleep. It felt so good.

Beep, beep, beep, beep!

I jumped up at the sound of Jaylen's alarm clock. It said 6:30 a.m. I went into the bathroom and took a shower. Luckily, I kept an extra outfit at Jaylen's house so I could go straight to work from here. Jaylen had to leave early this morning, so I didn't get a chance to see him. I got dressed and went into the kitchen to make some coffee. Jaylen had left me a note on the counter. It read: *I didn't want to wake you. You were sleeping like a baby. I'll be thinking about you all morning, and I'll see you this afternoon. Love, Jay.*

His little note made my morning. I smiled during the entire drive to work. I wanted to get an early start at the office today. Thank goodness, I didn't have to fight traffic this morning. It took me only thirty minutes to get to work.

I checked my machine, and I only had one message, from Roc. He wanted me to give him a call to discuss Damon.

Why does he want to talk to me about Damon? I thought

I dialed Roc's number, and his phone rang three times before he picked up.

"Talk to me," he said.

"Roc, it's me, Joi."

"Oh, my bad. I didn't realize that it was you."

"So what's up? What's going on with Damon?" I asked.

"Well, from what my sources tell me, Damon's attorney is trying to have his case thrown out. His attorney thinks he may have found a glitch in the system."

"Based on what?" I gasped.

"I'm not sure yet, Joi. I just wanted to give you an update. You know I got your back. When I get more information, I will give it to you."

"Okay. Just please keep me posted," I said.

"You don't even have to ask."

"Okay, I'll talk to you later, Roc. Thanks."

I hung up the telephone, and my nerves started to get the best of me. The mere mention of Damon's name sent shock waves through my body. If he got out, I didn't think I could handle it. I knew everything was too good to be true. I had had a lovely evening with Jaylen and a good morning, and now this.

"Calm down, Joi. He's not stupid enough to try anything. Even if he tried, Jaylen is here now, and he is not going to let anything happen to you," I told myself.

I took a small break to collect my thoughts and to get myself together. I felt like I was having a panic attack. After a while, I managed to get myself together, and I went back to my desk. I started working on some files, and before I knew it, it was 12:30 p.m. I gathered my things and left. I drove to Dr. Coleman's office, and when I pulled up, Jaylen was there waiting for me.

He walked over to my car and gave me a big hug and kiss.

"Joi, are you okay? You're trembling."

"I'll be fine, Jaylen. Let's just go inside."

"No, you are not fine. You were fine this morning, so I guess the question is what happened between then and now that has you all worked up and shaking?"

"Roc called me and told me that Damon's attorney might have found a glitch in the system to get him out of jail," I said.

"Is he absolutely sure?"

"I don't know, Jaylen, but what if Damon finds out that I was the one who turned him in? He's going to come after me."

"Well, he's going to have to come through me. I told you that I'm here to protect you, so don't worry your pretty little head over this punk. Let me handle this."

"Okay," I said.

Instantly, I calmed down, and I felt so much better. Having Jaylen in my life again made all the difference. We went inside Dr. Coleman's office at one thirty, as scheduled. Her receptionist advised her that we were in the waiting area.

"Dr. Coleman will see you now. You can go in the back," said the receptionist.

Jaylen and I got up to go in the back, to Dr. Coleman's office. We opened her door, and she stood up to greet us.

"Hello, Joi and Jaylen. It's nice to meet you both. Please have a seat on the couch."

Her office was decorated like somebody's living room. There was beautiful artwork on the walls, plants, and nice furniture. I looked around the room, admiring her decor. You could see all her degrees plastered on the wall.

"Would you like something to drink? We have bottled water, soda, and juice," said Dr. Coleman.

"We'll have two bottles of water please," I said.

"I would like to get started, so if you don't mind, I would like to ask both of you some questions," said Dr. Coleman. "Joi, are you an only child, and did you grow up with both of your parents present?"

"No, I am not an only child. I have a younger sister, and my parents are still married," I replied.

"Jaylen?" said Dr. Coleman.

"No, I have a brother, and my parents are still together," said Jaylen.

"Okay," Dr. Coleman said.

She started taking down notes and asking us more questions. She wanted to know about our goals, previous relationships, sibling relationships, and our professions, particularly why we chose them. I told her about Damon, and Jaylen told her about Toni. The entire session lasted for about an hour and forty-five minutes. She was very nice and thorough. Jaylen and I felt comfortable talking to her. Dr. Coleman wanted to know when could we come back in for another appointment. She wanted to review her notes so that we could get some answers to our questions. We scheduled another appointment for the following Tuesday at the same time. I just wanted to know if there was something wrong with me. We got up and left her office, holding hands.

"So, Jaylen, what did you think?" I asked as we walked to our cars.

"She seemed to be thorough. I don't think she missed a question."

"I know. Hopefully, next week we can get somewhere in terms of our relationship."

"Yeah, I agree."

Jaylen followed me to my house to pick up some clothes since I would be staying at his place for a couple of days. I was still a little shook up from Roc's telephone call. I went back to Jaylen's house, and I called Taj and Eboni. We all decided that we would take Faith out to the Cheesecake Factory. She loved that place. Everyone also chipped in to buy her a charm bracelet.

The rest of the week came and left. By Monday I was busy getting ready for my appointment the next day with Dr. Coleman and for Faith's graduation ceremony on Friday. I called Faith to see how she was holding up.

Ring . . .

"Hi, Faith. It's Joi."

"Hey, girl," Faith said, sounding exhausted.

"Is everything okay?"

"Yeah, I'm just tired. It's been a long weekend. So what's going on with you?"

"Nothing much," I said.

"How are the counseling sessions going?"

"They're going. We have a follow-up appointment tomorrow," I told her.

"Girl, you and Jaylen are fine. You just have issues, like everybody else. Look what I went through with that knucklehead Tyree. You live and you learn. So if she starts feeding you some psychological bullshit, don't feed into it. Shit, most of those doctors have issues that make yours look like nothing. Don't cosign the bull."

"You know I'm smarter than that. She seems to be cool. Jaylen and I are comfortable talking to her."

"Well, let me know what she said. Because if she is as cool as you say she is, I might just give her a try. Lord knows, I need some help."

"Okay. Well, I'll talk to you later."

"All right."

After that call, my day went by pretty fast. I left work and went straight to Jaylen's. I noticed that his car was there when I pulled up. To my surprise, when I opened the front door, I discovered he had a nice dinner waiting for me.

"Jaylen, you didn't have to do this for me," I told him.

"Here. These roses are for you."

"Thanks so much. They're beautiful. Let me put them in a vase."

"What are you doing home so early?"

"I wanted to make sure that you were all right," I said.

"Thanks, Joi. I love you."

"I love you, too."

This time I made him relax while I cleaned up. That night he gave me his bed while he slept on the couch.

The next day was routine. I went to work and left early for my appointment with Dr. Coleman. Today, she was going to tell Jaylen and me what our issues were. I met Jaylen in the parking lot at 1:25 p.m., and we walked into her office. The receptionist signed us in and called the doctor. We were instructed by the receptionist to go in to the doctor's office.

We opened Dr. Coleman's door, and she greeted us like before. "Hello, Joi and Jaylen. I'm so glad you could make it. Please have a seat on the couch."

"So Dr. Coleman, can you please give us some feedback as to why we made so many bad decisions in our previous relationships?" I said.

"Well, Joi, besides your being controlling and Jaylen being stubborn, you're fine. You're human, for crying out loud. We've all been where you were. What is important is that you both love each other and keep the lines of communication open. I swear, if half the people I see were as sane as you two, I would be out of business."

"So we're fine?" I asked.

"You're better than fine. Just take it slow and work through your problems together. The support has already been established. Pray for guidance, and don't worry about my fee. It's on the house."

Jaylen and I didn't know how to digest our diagnosis. But after replaying it in our heads over and over again, it finally dawned on us. We were meant to be with each other and not with other people. The foundation of our relationship had already been established a long time ago. We just needed to communicate more with each other. We had never stopped loving each other, and in some ways, it had made things difficult.

Jaylen found out that he was not the father of Toni's baby son through a paternity test. And speaking of tests, Jaylen and I got tested, and everything came back fine. I still thought about Damon every now and then, and as far as I knew, he was still locked up. I didn't worry about it like I had before, because Jaylen took such good care of me.

Epilogue

Joi

A year later . . .

Wow. I was getting married. I couldn't believe this was actually happening. I wore a Vera Wang gown that fit me perfectly! Yes, everybody stood up and watched as I, Joi Nicole, happily walked down the aisle to marry my soul mate, Jaylen. My father graciously gave me away as my mother tearfully watched. Taj, Eboni, and Gi'ana served as my bridesmaids, and Faith was my maid of honor.

We decided to say our own wedding vows straight from the heart. Neither of us read from a piece of paper. It just came naturally. Jay turned to me and held both of my hands.

"Joi, I love you with every fiber in me. I always have and always will love you, until the day I die. I want to laugh, cry, and build a family with you and just continue to be your best friend. I will always cherish and respect you for the beautiful human being you are. I love you and thank you for being you. Thank you, God, for blessing me with such an angel."

By now, everyone was crying, including me. Jaylen definitely took it there. Now it was my turn.

"Jaylen, for as long as I've known you, from the moment I laid eyes on you, I've loved you. I never thought in a million years I could find someone who could brighten my world, my spirit, and my heart. I promise to cherish each and every moment with you, and to share a family and a loving relationship. I promise you that I will always be by your side through the good and bad times. My heart skips a beat whenever I see you or hear your voice. When we are apart, you are with me everywhere I go. Mentally, you stay on my mind twenty-four hours a day; emotionally, you are my rock; and physically, you far exceed all my needs. I truly believe that we are soul mates, and I could not have been blessed with a better person to share my life with, because you complete me." Tears rolled down my cheeks.

"Baby, I told you not to cry," said Jaylen.

"Aaww!" the guests said simultaneously.

"May I please have the rings," the pastor requested.

After he blessed the rings, we exchanged them.

"By the powers vested in me, I now pronounce you husband and wife. You may kiss your bride," said the pastor.

Gi'ana lifted my veil over my face, and Jaylen kissed me like never before. Everyone was clapping.

"So without further adieu, I give to you Mr. and Mrs. Jaylen Payne," said the pastor.

This time Jay and I both cried happy tears as we released the doves into the air. Everyone clapped again.

Everyone started walking down the aisle. I was smiling, and Jay was giving any and everybody a high five, which was his thing. I had invited Craig to the wedding, but he had declined, sending his well wishes. Lex had wanted my aunt and uncle to raise Brandon, so that was where he went. Craig moved an hour away, with his girlfriend, Elisha. I thought it was a little tacky on his part, but he had been tacky about his marriage for a while now, so I wasn't surprised. He sent money for Brandon and came to visit him often. He would take him to Aunt Alexis's burial site on special holidays, which I thought was nice.

I noticed a familiar face in the crowd, but I could not make sense of who it was, because the male figure kept disappearing into the crowd. All of a sudden, I had this weird feeling in my stomach. I decided to let it go and continue enjoying my moment with the love of my life.

However, as I passed Roc, he gave me a note, which read: *I tried to reach you earlier to let you know that Damon was released from jail, and that he knows you turned him in. I don't mean to mess up your wedding day. I thought you needed to know. I'm doing what I need to do, so don't worry. I think I saw him here. Be careful.*

Discussion Questions

1. Considering the relationship that Joi and Jaylen had in the past, was it a good idea for Joi to attend Jaylen and Toni's wedding? Why or why not?

2. The five girlfriends come from various economic and social backgrounds. What do these women have in common that enables them to maintain such a close bond? Have you personally lost a friendship because your goals and dreams differed from those of a friend? Share this experience with the group.

3. Why does Faith avoid Tina when it comes to going to church?

4. What strength can you derive from reflecting on Alexis's situation?

5. What are some bad signs that Faith recognized or should have recognized in her relationship with Tyree? Give some examples. Did you think he was married?

6. In the book, Taj and Eboni seem insignificant to a certain degree. Even though that was not the intention, name a group (rap or R & B) in which an individual or individuals appear somewhat unimportant yet share a bond or closeness with others in the group.

7. What meaning do you think the author is conveying with the title *Finding Joy In Pain*? How does it tie in to Joi and Jaylen's situation?

8. Damon comes off as a secure, intelligent, and successful young man who could probably have anyone he wanted. Why is he so attached to Joi? Is he actually insecure? If so, why? What do you think caused him to become a stalker and rapist?

9. Alexis and Joi seem really close. Their relationship seems to be one of love and respect. Do you share the same closeness with a family member or friend? If so, what component in that relationship keeps it all together?

10. In the book, there are two people (male and female) who really connect. Who are they, and could they ever be a couple? Explain your answer.

11. Out of all the main characters, who reminds you the most of yourself? Why?

12. What do you like most about Joi's character? What do you dislike most about Joi's character?

13. In your own opinion, which famous actresses and actors could play Alexis and Craig, Joi and Jaylen, and Faith and Tyree?

14. Should Joi have married Jaylen when he asked her years ago? Explain your answer.

15. What do you think of Toni? Do you believe she loved Jaylen from the beginning? Do you believe Jaylen loved her from the beginning?